D1164481

"LORD, you establish peace for us;
all that we have accomplished you have done for
us."

Isaiah 26:12 (NIV)

CONTENTS

Exodus 14:14
Ian Vroon

EMMANUEL

The Life of Jesus Dramatized

Bible Study Guide Included

God With Us

IAN VROON

Copyright © 2020 by Ian Vroon

All rights reserved. This book or any portion thereof may not be reproduced or used in any manner whatsoever without the express written permission of the author except for the use of brief quotations. For permission requests, write to the author, addressed "Attention: "Permissions" at the address below.

First Edition, 2020

ISBN: 9798651286263
Imprint: Independently published

All Scripture quotations, unless otherwise indicated, are taken from the Holy Bible, New International Version®. NIV®. Copyright © 1973, 1978, 1984 by International Bible Society. Used by permission of Zondervan. All rights reserved.

Ordering Information for Quantity Sales:
Special discounts are available on quantity purchases (20 or more). For details contact Ian Vroon on his blog.

Find Ian on his blog at
http://Isaiah2612.weebly.com

Cover art by
Tony Melena

01 • A Voice in the Desert

John 1:1-34

In the beginning was the Word.

"Repent!"

Crowds gathered near the Jordan River. A man stood in it with outstretched arms and pleading eyes. "Repent," he repeated, "for the Kingdom is near."

The people murmured to each other. Who was this guy? Why was he speaking with such authority? And what did he mean by "repent"? Had they committed some great sin?

"Repent of your sins! Be baptized." The man beckoned with both hands, eyes wild as he implored his audience. "Your sins will be forgiven."

No one stirred, but all were watching—looking up and down the shore, waiting for someone to move. Whispers swept through the crowd. Could this man be serious?

*And the Word was with God, and the
Word was God. He was with God in the
beginning.*

Timidly, a man stepped forward. There was a ripple where his toes broke the water—then his feet were submerged, and his shaking knees pushed him further into the river. He raised both arms to steady himself, stumbled forward—the water's chill made him wince—and with a few splashes came up to his waist.

The man preaching repentance watched hopefully, reaching out as the volunteer reached him. "Yes, yes!" The Baptist clapped his new convert on the shoulder and nodded triumphantly. "Now repent of your sins and I will baptize you."

The man exhaled slowly, folding his hands and watching the sky. "I repent," he said weakly. "I have been a foolish and stubborn man." He closed his eyes. "I need forgiveness."

Without hesitation, the Baptist plunged him underwater. Water exploded a second later as he pulled his convert up, spraying the Jordan's surface with shimmering sunlight. The man inhaled quickly and shook his head.

"Well done." The Baptist's eyes gleamed with tears. "Produce fruit in keeping with repentance." He patted him on the shoulder, then turned toward the shore. "Who's next?"

*Through him all things were made;
without him nothing was made that has
been made.*

"He calls himself John."

"His name is John? But isn't he Zechariah's son?"

"An angel named him, if the rumors are true."

A Levite in the group scoffed. "These self-proclaimed prophets," he spat, looking toward the river. "What authority does he have to baptize? He wears a leather belt and clothing made of camel's hair like he's Elijah—and he comes from the desert. Probably half mad from the heat."

"But what if he is Elijah?"

The Levite shook his head. "Impossible. We Jews don't need baptism. If he were Elijah, he would know that—instead of treating us like uncircumcised Gentiles."

The other priest disagreed. "This man is different," he insisted, glancing at the shore. "The people take him very seriously, and we should do the same."

"Perhaps."

"Perhaps?" His friend raised both eyebrows. He pointed toward the river, where an explosion of water marked John's eighth convert in the last fifteen minutes. "A week ago, people were afraid to go near him. Now the entire countryside is lining up to hear him." He lifted his chin. "For a crazed man, he's awfully persuasive."

"He certainly has a strong spirit—but not all spirits are the Holy Spirit."

"Granted," he replied, and shrugged. "But why not give him a chance? Ask him."

"Very well," the Levite said, turning to leave. "We will gather a group."

Those nearby murmured in excitement. Soon they would discover if this John the Baptist was Elijah, the Prophet or—possibly—the Christ.

For why else did their hearts burn within them?

In him was life, and that life was the light of men.

† † †

Over four hundred years earlier

"You call this a sacrifice?" Malachi's staff poked the crippled lamb one man had brought in. "Do you actually—" he leapt forward, "Do you think God is pleased with the worst of your flock?"

The man shied back, dropping his lamb. "I want to bring an—an offering to the Lord—"

Malachi raised a finger to silence the man. "This," he breathed, "Is what *YHWH Sabaoth*—the Lord Almighty— says:

"A son honors his father, and a servant his master. If I am a father, where is the honor due me? If I am a master, where is the respect due me?"

"But—"

"But you ask—" Malachi made his voice whiny and high-pitched to imitate the priests—"'How have we shown contempt for you?'"

He stamped the ground with his staff, and the nearby priests recoiled. "By sacrificing crippled and diseased animals!" He kicked the defective lamb on the floor. "Try offering these to your governor and see what he thinks!"

Now the priests were visibly shaken. They took a few steps back, but the Lord's messenger pursued them. "My name—says the Lord Almighty—is to be great among the nations. Great!" Malachi glared at them. "From the rising to the setting of the sun."

The priests were backed into the wall now. "We—we light fires on the altar—"

"Useless fires!" Spittle flew from Malachi's mouth. "The Lord Almighty is not pleased with you—and he will accept no offering from your hands."

One of them protested. "But our festival sacrifices—"

"I will spread on your faces the *animal entrails* from your sacrifices!" Malachi's hand made a covering motion over the priest's face. "And you will be carried outside the temple and *burned* with it."

The priest's mouth opened—then he swallowed. "We—"

"I remember my covenant with Levi—says the Lord Almighty." Malachi gave a little smile. "A covenant of life and peace." He breathed in deeply, closing his eyes. "He stood in awe of my name—and true instruction was on his lips. He walked with me in peace and righteousness, and turned many from sin."

His eyes flew open. "But you—you!" He thrust a trembling finger at them. "*You* have violated the covenant of your fathers. You have turned from God's way and your teaching has led others astray. You have broken faith!"

"We didn't mean to! It's just—it's been so long." The priest's lower lip trembled. He held out his hands. "Where is the prosperity Yahweh promised us? We returned from exile long ago."

Malachi studied him, knuckles white as he clutched his staff. Then he gave a long, drawn out sigh. "This admonition is for *your* sake," he emphasized. "For the sake of my covenant with Levi—and because I love you."

Another priest found his tongue. "But—but how?!"

"By choosing you over Esau," Malachi replied. "I transformed Edom's mountains into a desert wasteland—a haunt for jackals."

"But what's the use?" The first priest pleaded with his hands. "God has abandoned us. We are a downtrodden nation under oppression. We pray to him and he doesn't listen." He shook his head. "Why bother? His promises are not coming true."

The other priests murmured in agreement, nodding to each other. "Where is the eternal kingdom he promised?" one of them asked. "Where is the Messiah come to judge the world?"

Malachi rolled his eyes. "You flood the altar with tears!" he spat. "You weep and wail and ask, 'Why?'" He pointed at their faces. "It is because you have broken faith with the wife of your youth and married the daughters of foreign gods. You have divorced and you have ignored the covenant."

No reply. None of them could meet his eyes.

Malachi leaned into their faces. "You have wearied the Lord with your words." He bobbed his head from side to side and imitated their speech. "But you ask, 'How have we wearied him?'"

Malachi stamped the ground with his staff. "By saying it is futile to serve God! You ask where the God of justice is. But the Lord does not change." His shoulders lowered. "That is why he still loves you."

He beckoned with his free hand. "Return to him, and he will return to you."

The priests whispered to each other, uneasy but receptive. One of them cleared his throat. "And the Messiah?"

Malachi smiled. "This is the Lord Almighty's answer:

"See, I will send my messenger, who will prepare the way before me." Malachi straightened. "Then suddenly the Lord you are seeking will come to his temple; the messenger of the covenant, whom you desire, will come."

✝   ✝   ✝

The Present

The light shines in the darkness, but the darkness has not understood it.

There he was. John the Baptist, Elijah's twin, passionately exhorting the crowd toward repentance. The crowds were thicker than ever, drawn by the promise of forgiveness.

The Pharisees and Sadducees also sought baptism. After all, it was the proper thing to do. They approached the shore tentatively, letting the crowd part before them.

John saw them and his eyes grew wide. "You brood of vipers!" he screamed, throwing a trembling finger in their direction. "Who warned you to flee from the coming wrath?"

The crowd gasped. The Pharisees and Sadducees exchanged glances—had they just heard that?

"And don't you even think about saying 'We have Abraham as our father'!" John's voice shook with fury. He jabbed his finger at a nearby cluster of rocks. "I tell you that out of these *stones* God can raise up children for Abraham."

This was unacceptable. Who did this man think he was? The Lord's messenger? Not since Malachi had they been so vehemently—

"The ax is already at the root of the tree," John continued, making a sinister motion with his hands. "And every tree that does not bear good fruit will be cut down—" he clenched his fist, "And thrown into the fire."

The people were speechless. Some turned to the Pharisees and Sadducees—but their mouths were open, hands hanging by their sides.

Then a woman broke from the crowd. "What should we do?" She fell to her knees, holding out her hands. "What *can* we do?"

Anxious murmurs rippled through the crowd. What would John say?

"The man with two tunics should share with him who has none," John replied, "and the one who has food should do the same."

Some in the crowd murmured approval. A few tax collectors stepped out and asked, "Teacher, what about us?"

John indicated the crowd with his palm. "Don't collect more money than you have to."

"And us?" A soldier approached him with two of his comrades. He dipped his head to John in respect. "What should *we* do?"

"Don't extort people and don't accuse people falsely." John's eyes blazed as he surveyed the soldiers. "Be content with your pay."

The soldier swallowed. "Right," he said, stepping into the water, "It will be as you say."

John nodded. "Make your words your life."

> *There came a man who was sent from*
> *God; his name was John. He came as a*
> *witness to testify concerning that light, so*
> *that through him all men might believe.*

"There he is." The priests and Levites made their way toward the shore, whispering to each other. "John the Baptist—our supposed Elijah."

A Levite scoffed. "He certainly plays the part."

"I hear he eats locusts and wild honey."

"Grew up in the Qumran community, I think. Been living in the desert for years."

"Qumran? Aren't they all crazy?"

John's words floated over the water: "He who comes after me has surpassed me, because he was before me!"

Yep. Completely mad.

"John the Baptist!"

John turned to see the priests and Levites approaching the water's edge. His face became stone.

"We have some questions for you." One of the priests cleared his throat. "The people wish to know who you are."

John's expression did not change. "Fire away."

The priest cleared his throat. "Are you the Christ?"

The crowd waited with bated breath. Was this it?

John spread his arms. "I am not the Christ," he confessed, dipping his head.

There were murmurs. Not the Christ?

"Then who are you?" The priest tilted his head. "Are you Elijah?"

"I am not."

More murmurs. The priest glanced at his comrades, but they only shrugged. "Are you the Prophet?"

"No."

A moment of silence. Then, "Well who are you?"

No reply. John stared at him, eyes burning.

"Give us *something* to take back to those who sent us." The priest pleaded with his hands. "What do you say about yourself?"

John raised his face toward heaven and closed his eyes. "I am the voice of one calling in the desert." He spread his arms. "Make straight the way for the Lord."

The priests whispered to each other. The words of Isaiah the prophet?

"Every valley will be filled in, every mountain made low," John continued, "The crooked roads will become straight, the rough ways smooth." He opened his eyes. "Then all mankind will see God's salvation."

The true light that gives life to every man
was coming into the world.

"Strong words from Isaiah."

The crowd turned to see a Pharisee making his way toward John. He stopped at the shore and sneered. "But you are not Elijah. And you are not the Prophet." He raised his chin. "And you are certainly no Messiah."

Other Pharisees gathered behind him. No doubt they had arrived with the priests.

"I preach repentance," John replied, "to prepare the path for the Messiah."

"Oh?" The Pharisee arched an eyebrow. "And just how does baptizing people do that?"

John cupped water in both hands. "It cleanses their hearts." He opened his fingers, letting the liquid trickle between them. "Allowing the Messiah passage." He pointed at the people. "*They* are his path."

The Word became flesh and made his dwelling among us.

Feet moved behind the crowd, dust rising with each step. Another man had joined.

"I baptize with water," John said, cupping water with one hand. "But among you stands one you do not know—one more powerful than I."

The feet moved through the crowd slowly, dust turning to sand.

"One whose sandals I am not worthy to untie." He dumped the water this time, inhaling deeply. "He will baptize with the Holy Spirit—" he gritted his teeth, "and with fire."

The feet reached the river's edge and stopped.

"His winnowing fork is in his hand, and he will clear his threshing floor," John continued, making a motion with his hands. "He'll gather the wheat into his barn—and *burn* the chaff with unquenchable fire."

A man stepped forward. There was a ripple where his toes broke the water—then his feet were submerged. He moved with purpose, and the crowd watched as he approached John. The Baptist had stopped speaking, and now all eyes were on the newcomer.

The man crossed his arms over his chest. "I am ready," he said, keeping his eyes fixed on John. "Baptize me."

John found his tongue. "Jesus! I remember you!" He creased his eyebrows, trying to place a memory. "What are you doing here? *I* need to be baptized by *you!*" He shook his head, incredulous. "And you come to me?"

Jesus nodded. "We must do this to fulfill every righteous requirement."

John closed his mouth, studying the man's face. He remembered his friend from childhood, but that was it. From what he could tell, Jesus was still more righteous than he would ever be. But if the friend wanted John to baptize him—

"Very well," John said, taking Jesus in his arms. The surface broke as he thrust the man through it. A second spent underwater—

> *The prophet Isaiah stood before the people of Israel, long robes and staff. He held out a hand to indicate an unseen friend. "Here is my servant, whom I uphold," he said softly, "my chosen one in whom I delight." He smiled confidently. "I will put my Spirit on him—and he will bring justice to the nations."*

—An explosion of water droplets preceded Jesus' exit. The man from Galilee inhaled sharply and cleared his eyes. John clapped him on the shoulder—

And the heavens opened.

Far above the river, beyond the stars, beyond the whirling galaxies and cosmos, through the black holes and nebulae and voids of deep space, there is a throne. Above all majesties and powers and kings and queens this throne rests. The Earth is its footstool—the roots of the mountains trinkets at its base.

From it rules an eternal power, an omnipotent being wrapped in light and zeal as a cloak, bearing righteousness as a breastplate and salvation as a helmet, and holding the fate of every creature in his right hand. Before the past, after the future, and greater than the present, he reigns with an outstretched arm and a mighty fist.

His wrath is poured out like fire—and shatters the rocks before him. Mountains melt beneath him like wax running from a candle. Valleys split apart from his anger. The trenches of the ocean are laid bare at his rebuke.

His love redeems nations. What is torn and shattered is restored, piece by fragment, until it is superior to its original. The adulteress is allured by his love. The valley of trouble becomes a door of hope with his guidance. He cares for any who would trust in him, and he heals all who would come to him.

He is God.

Now the Holy Spirit descends to the Earth. The Earth, that infinitesimal speck in an infinite cosmos. No small cause sends him there. The Holy Spirit is on a mission.

Past every galaxy, through the atmosphere and to a small river between continents. He assumes the form of a white bird, simple and sublime—a dove. Peace. He flutters more slowly now, descending upon the man exiting the water.

God's Son.

It is a mission older than time—and the time has come for its accomplishment.

A voice shook the Jordan River and thundered across the sky.

"This is my Son, whom I love."

Jesus raised his arms to receive the Holy Spirit, now a dove descending upon him.

"With him I am well pleased."

The crowd was speechless. Jesus exited the river, streams of water cascading down his tunic as he shook his sandaled feet.

"Look!" John said, pointing at Jesus, "The Lamb of God who takes away the sin of the world!" He looked around the crowd with wild eyes, gesturing frantically. "Don't talk about me! I'm not the messiah! I was sent to prepare the way and to reveal the One who will walk it. The One on whom the Holy Spirit rests!" He sloshed through the Jordan, unable to control himself. "I have seen," he stammered, almost tripping. "I have seen and I testify!"

He reached the shore in a few steps and stopped. Pointing a shaking finger at Jesus, he said, "I have seen and I testify that this is the Messiah—the Son of God!"

> *We have seen his glory, the glory of the*
> *One and Only, who came from the*
> *Father, full of grace and truth.*

02 • THE TEMPTATION OF JESUS

MATTHEW 4:1-11; LUKE 4:1-13

By the Father's command, there was one remaining task for Jesus before he could begin his ministry on this Earth—one crucial thing. Human and divine, strong in the Spirit yet vulnerable in the flesh, he retreated to the desert alone.

It was a test—a trial.

Heat rose from the desert in waves. Jesus sat on a rock with head in hands, breathing deeply. Before him a lion growled—but did not approach.

A snake slithered past Jesus' feet. He did not turn or lift up his head, but exhaled. The sun beat down on his neck and hands. Sweat trickled down his cheek, and he licked his cracked lips.

"He doesn't love you."

A voice, sickeningly sweet, whispering in Jesus' ear. Jesus lifted his head, eyes half-closed. It hurt to swallow.

"He will not provide for you."

A hot wind stirred the nearby sand—and it became a small tornado, which dissipated at Jesus' feet.

The well-dressed man sitting beside him had smooth skin and a pleasant smile. His voice was like silk. "You are abandoned."

A whisper of a cough from Jesus. He dipped his head, trying to wet his lips again. His hands were beginning to peel.

"You must be hungry."

Jesus reached unsteadily for the flask of water on his lap. He opened it with trembling fingers, then raised it to his lips.

"Forty days," the man said, standing up. He walked a few feet, then stooped down. "Forty days without food. Must feel like forty years."

Jesus swallowed the water—then gasped in relief as it washed down his throat. He set the flask on a rock.

His tormentor stood, stone in hand. "This," he presented the stone to Jesus, "is your salvation."

Jesus stared at him, silent.

Satan turned the stone in his hands, watching it with exaggerated interest. "To most people, this would just be a stone." He caught Jesus' eye and smiled. "But you are the Son of God." He tossed the stone and caught it. "To you this stone is bread."

Jesus's eyes settled on the rock. He swallowed.

"Just say the word," the man lowered his voice, "—and the meal is yours."

Jesus' face was expressionless. His mouth slowly opened, but he remained silent.

Satan gripped the stone tighter. "You have no choice!" he spat, suddenly indignant. "Your God will not provide for you! You must provide for yourself!" He gritted his teeth. "He has abandoned you."

✝   ✝   ✝

2nd Millennium BC

Forty years in the desert. Forty long years and before that, no one knew. The sand, the wind, the brush and occasional mountain—this was their world.

But now they were entering the Promised Land.

The Israelites stood before Moses. Livestock bleating, children crying, mothers hushing, fathers attempting to restore order, others coughing—the beginnings of a proud nation. No one to show them the way into the promised land except their mighty leader—and he was forbidden from entering by the God they all served.

It would be a very long day.

Moses now recited the law to them. His voice boomed across the gathering, authority punctuating each syllable. "Be careful to follow every command I am giving you today," he said, "so that you may live and increase and may enter and possess the land that the Lord promised on oath to your forefathers."

Those forefathers had disobeyed. Now their children stood ready to receive the promise. If Moses wasn't clear enough: *don't you blow it too.*

"Remember how the Lord your God led you all the way in the desert these forty years—" there were some murmurs and uneasy shuffling in the crowd—"to humble you and to test you in order to know what was in your heart, whether or not you would keep his commands." He cleared his throat. "He humbled you, causing you to hunger—and then feeding you."

The crowd murmured louder, some casting angry glances in Moses' direction. Oh, they remembered. That delightful manna. Fell from heaven every day, never to be saved except before the Sabbath. Every week for forty years they remembered.

Moses silenced them with his hand. "He did this to teach you," he said firmly. "To teach you that man does not live on bread alone—" he pointed at the heavens—"but on every word that comes from the mouth of God."

✝ ✝ ✝

The Present

Jesus spoke. "It is written." Though faint, his voice carried conviction. "Man does not live on bread alone."

The stone dropped to the sand.

"Very well," Satan sneered, grasping Jesus's shoulder. The ground fell from their feet as they ascended, and a pleasant breeze rippled their garments. Sun was obscured by clouds and desert replaced by Jerusalem. Under them flew markets, soldiers, passages and carts—then they arrived. Upon the pinnacle they alighted.

The Temple of Jerusalem.

"Ah, yes," Satan said, gesturing at the people below. "This is your Father's house."

Jesus remained silent.

The devil took on an apologetic tone. "You know, I haven't been fair with you." He walked around to Jesus' other side. "I haven't given you the respect you deserve."

Jesus swallowed, raising his chin.

"I have not acknowledged your indisputable knowledge of the Scriptures." Now a gleam entered Satan's eye. "But why should I pretend to be different?" He spread his arms. "After all, I too love the Scriptures."

Jesus exhaled slowly, closing his eyes.

"That is why I took you here." The devil's eyebrows creased piously. "I attend the Temple worship on *Shabbat* too. Faithfully. In fact, every day I am there." He smiled wickedly. "In the hearts and minds of the teachers and their aspiring pupils."

Jesus kept his eyes closed.

"You doubt me?" Satan feigned offense. "Well! I certainly didn't expect that from the Son of God!" He shook his head. "I need to demonstrate for you."

He put his arm on Jesus' shoulder and walked him to the edge. A gust of wind stirred Jesus' hair—the valley was hundreds of feet below.

"Now this is an excellent opportunity to test the promises of the good Lord," he said jovially, patting Jesus on the shoulder. He kicked some dust off the edge and watched it fall to the ground below. "Throw yourself down."

Jesus surveyed the valley, eyes half-lidded.

"Come on," Satan said, nudging him gently, "you know you won't get hurt." He held up a finger. "For it is written, 'He will command his angels concerning you, and they will lift you up in their hands—'" he made a scooping motion with his hands, "'so that you will not strike your foot against a stone.'"

Satan stepped back and sighed in satisfaction. "See? Scripture."

Jesus inhaled deeply.

"Well surely you don't doubt God's provision, do you?" Satan's eyes widened. "I mean, look where we are: his very temple!" He indicated Jesus energetically. "And look who you are! You're the Son of God!" He put his hands on his hips. "You are so sure God will provide for you and watch over you." The devil pointed to the valley below. "Then prove it."

† † †

2nd Millennium BC

"We're going to die out here!"

Rephidim was not exactly a reservoir of water, and the people knew it. Now the elders pleaded with Moses for their lives, scraping at his feet and clenching their fists.

"Stop this," Moses said sharply. "The Lord will provide. Look at the manna."

Even now, white flakes were falling from the sky gently, coating an entire race with nourishment for the day's journey.

"But water!"

"Don't worry. Don't be afraid."

"We'll die of thirst!"

Moses sighed. "Why? Why do you quarrel with me?" He threw up his hands. "Why do you put the Lord to the test?"

One of them shook his head. "I should be asking you why," he began, getting to his feet. "Why you led us out here." He shoved his finger in Moses' face. "So that we can die? So that our children can die? So that our livestock can die?" He spun to the people. "So that we can all die of thirst!"

Protests rippled through the crowd. Moses had betrayed them! He'd failed to provide for them! His God had let them down! If they'd just stayed in Egypt, they would have plenty to drink now.

Moses retreated behind a rock. The elders raised their fists and shouted, chanting, "Water! Water! Is the Lord among us or not?"

"God," he whispered, "What do I do? These people are about ready to stone me!"

The crowd took up the chant. One of the elders went up by the rock and yelled, "Come on, Moses! Does your God care for us or not?"

Moses closed his eyes. "Thank you, Lord," he said, leaning on his staff. "Now give me the strength to obey you." He stepped out from behind the rock and indicated the elders. "Come with me."

The elders stopped chanting, exchanging victorious glances. Now they would see. That God of Moses would prove he cared for them. He would show his power.

That, or they would die of thirst.

Moses walked ahead of them, marking each step with his staff. Would they never learn?

An enormous boulder loomed before them: The Rock of Horeb. Barren and hard as they came. Flat, unbreakable.

Perfect for displaying the power of God.

Moses stood next to the rock and cleared his throat. "Watch and see," he declared, "the Lord your God always provides."

The elders scoffed. What was he talking about? There was no water here. The man must be hallucinating.

But what the elders did not see was the other man standing by the rock. The Lord stood with tears in his eyes, watching them. *Why?* His voice went unheard. *Why don't you trust me?*

Moses bit his lip. *God, I trust you. I trust you enough to carry out even this command.*

But why don't they? The Lord held his palm out. *Don't they know how much I love them? Didn't I prove it when I brought them up out of Egypt?* A tear flowed down his cheek. *I feed them with manna every day! I care for them more than they care for themselves!* He stretched out both hands, pleading. *Israel, why don't you trust me?*

Moses raised his staff to carry out the Lord's command. The elders watched with bated breath, waiting for proof that God really cared for them.

The staff struck the rock, bouncing off. No wooden staff could ever penetrate such stone—

Slowly, cracks formed in the surface where the staff had struck. Jagged valleys penetrated the rock like lightning in a stormy sky. Stone crumbled and disintegrated from the impact point, tumbling to the dirt.

And then, with a thunderous roar, came water.

A flood of it—too much for the men to drink. Pure and clean, it became a rushing torrent, fleeing the broken rock and emptying into a gorge.

The elders were speechless. How could this be?

Slowly but steadily, Moses lowered his staff, as drained as the rock beside him. He sighed. "Now do you believe?"

† † †

The Present

Jesus shook his head. "It is also written: 'Do not put the Lord your God to the test.'"

Satan snarled—then they were off again, beyond city, desert, river and plain. Clouds began to clear as they ascended, and specks of green became trees as the face of their destination approached. A mountainside loomed before them.

Chill winds snapped at them as they rose—and they flew over springs and carpets of flowers. Snow flurried around them, stinging Jesus's cheeks as they shot over the peak.

On the snow they descended. It crunched beneath their feet as they landed. A vast panorama lay before them.

"Welcome," Satan said, "to my kingdom."

Jesus turned to find his tormentor—the prince of this world—clothed in flowing robes, a golden scepter caressed in one hand.

"We should be honest," the devil said, tilting his head. "The road you are about to walk will be unimaginably difficult the whole way." He leaned in, lips curling back. "And I will oppose you at every turn." He paced to Jesus' other side. "You will be flogged, beaten, mocked, tempted in every way. You will sweat blood and tears. You will be tortured," he whispered, enunciating each syllable, "and bear every piece of hatred your people have ever felt on your shoulders."

Jesus swallowed.

"You will know pain," Satan breathed, "and I will make you suffer until you beg for another path." He held his fist before Jesus. "Nails will pierce your skin, those you love most will reject and betray you!" The fist shook with rage. "And I will be there for every blow."

Jesus inhaled deeply, staring ahead.

"I will see to it myself that you suffer the most excruciating death imaginable." He smiled wickedly. "I will destroy you."

Then the prince shrugged. "So why bother? Ah yes," he snickered, "your Father has promised you something, hasn't he?" He rolled his eyes. "Dominion over all the kingdoms of the world. Set under your feet."

Jesus gave an almost imperceptible nod.

Satan shook his head. "Ah, but I already have all the kingdoms of the world. They were given to me by your Father." Now the devil indicated Jesus, eyes gleaming. "And I can give them to anyone I want to. So I can give you a shortcut—a much easier way." He stretched his scepter toward the panorama. As Jesus looked, a whirl of images played across it.

Legions of Roman soldiers marching in perfect unison, called to a distant battle.

Egyptian horses galloping across a plain, pulling chariots and armored drivers.

Showers of arrows from Macedonian archers across a darkened field.

A vast empire of aqueducts and roads running across the world. Caravans with delicacies and spices, perfumes and dyes.

Harems and slave women dancing for an emperor. Rich feasts and extravagant baths, servants standing by for the next command.

Temples with ancient altars and incense burning to an unknown god. Enormous statues of gold and silver. Columns of granite.

The kingdoms of the world.

"Everything anyone could ever want," the devil said, grinning. "And it's all yours."

Jesus stood silently in the wind, cloak flapping. The montage continued, but he looked toward heaven.

"I can give you all of this," Satan offered, "all their authority and splendor. Yours." He leaned in close as if whispering a secret. "No sacrifice needed. You won't have to suffer one bit. You can have it *all* right now without the pain and torment."

Jesus closed his eyes.

"The catch, well—" Satan chuckled, tapping his palm with the scepter, "it's not really a catch. It's nothing, really."

The tempter strolled over to Jesus's other side, putting a hand on his shoulder. With his other hand he pointed the scepter at Jesus's heart. "All you have to do," he said, moving the scepter to himself, "is bow down and worship me."

Satan smiled and stepped back. He spread his arms wide. "Well?" he asked, watching the Son of God. "What do you say? You'd have to be a *fool* to choose the other road."

Faintly, as a whisper in Jesus' mind, Isaiah's voice carried over the centuries:

I the Lord have called you in righteousness;
I will take hold of your hand.
I will keep you and will make you
To be a covenant for the people
And a light for the Gentiles,
To open eyes that are blind,
To free captives from prison
And to release from the dungeon those who sit in darkness.

"Away from me, Satan!" Jesus shouted, waving a hand. "For it is written: 'Worship the Lord your God, and serve him only.'"

Satan's scepter cracked. The prince of darkness stared at Jesus, incredulous. "You—" he swallowed suddenly, then bared his teeth. "Very well." He turned with a flourish of his robe, darkness shrouding him. "You have won." His form vanished, but a faint whisper penetrated the wind. "For now."

Instantly Jesus was back in the desert. He looked around slowly—the sun forced him to squint—and spotted water flask on the rock. He stepped toward it, but his knees collapsed. With a groan, Jesus fell to the ground.

Sand rose by his face. Two pairs of sandaled feet stood beside him. He rolled onto his back, looking up to see his rescuers.

Two men stood dressed in white linen. They stooped and, carefully lifting Jesus in their arms, walked him to a nearby rock. He lay face up on the stone, eyes half-closed.

"Eat," one of them said, procuring a loaf of bread from thin air.

The Lamb of God stared at it. The bread glowed white in the sun, and he took it with a trembling hand. Then he tried to sit up, and the angels pulled his arms until he was upright. Calmly he broke the bread.

"Thank you, Father," he whispered, raising a piece to his mouth. He took a bite, chewed, took another bite—and his strength began to return. "You have provided, as always."

A few feet away from him lay a stone, untouched, unmoved.

03 • TOO SMALL A THING

JOHN 4:1-42

Circa 760 BC

So they'd repented.

Jonah stood by the city gates, running a hand through his hair. Insufferable—wicked, vile wretches! Deserving of the torment and destruction that only the Almighty could ladle out.

He turned to leave, crossing under the archway. He was done with Nineveh.

"Lord." The words barely escaped his clenched teeth. A trembling whisper at best. "Isn't this what I said when I was at home? This is *exactly* why I fled to Tarshish." He pounded his palm with a fist. "Exactly why!"

No response. He supposed God was content to let him rant.

"This is just like you, Yahweh." Jonah quickened his pace. "Gracious and compassionate, slow to anger—

abounding in love. You love relenting from sending calamity. That's your thing."

Still no response. Jonah shook his head, teeth clenched. "You can't just bring justice, can you! You have to forgive too!"

Jonah.

God's voice. Jonah stopped on the path leading out of the city, eyes turned to the sky. Yahweh was always listening. "I have a request, Yahweh."

Silence. Jonah swallowed, balling his fists. He'd felt this rage building for hours—but there was nothing he could do with it. Not without sinning against the Creator. "I can't live with what you've done here. You are just, you are holy—I can't charge you with wrongdoing. But I can't accept this!"

Still no response. The sun beat down on him, the sky cloudless.

"I *won't* accept this!" Jonah was screaming, his jowls shaking. "Kill me now! I'd rather die! That would be better misery than watching Nineveh live."

Have you any right to be angry?

Jonah blinked. His fists loosened—and he swallowed. No sense arguing with El Shaddai.

No, his best course was to head for that hill. Sit on it, watch the city—see what happened. Maybe Yahweh would punish Nineveh after all. Or maybe he would grant Jonah's request and kill him.

Either way, couldn't hurt.

✝   ✝   ✝

Still nothing. Jonah had been watching for the whole forty days.

The people were still wearing sackcloth and ashes, course—the idiot Ninevites had even draped goatskin over their cows, for crying out loud. What a bunch of fools. As if cows could repent in dust and ashes.

But it was the idea, of course. They were repenting—and to the Israelite God. Yahweh was being glorified.

But didn't justice also bring Yahweh glory?

At least Jonah had this gourd vine. A massive leaf cast shade on his head and back. The sun was no laughing matter—and even at dawn, this time of year was hot.

Sunlight shone in his eyes. He squinted up at the leaf. Was that a hole? Really?

Great. So something was chewing the leaf. An aphid, perhaps? Who knew.

Jonah closed his eyes, expelling a trembling breath. Was Yahweh mocking him? This vine had grown up in just the right spot—clearly a provision from God. But now something was eating it.

That was no coincidence.

✝ ✝ ✝

Well. It was official. The leaf was gone. Jonah squinted up at its tattered shreds, raising a palm to shield his eyes. Sweat trickled down his temple, tracing his jawline. It was painful to swallow. The sun was right in the center of the sky, bringing up waves of shimmering heat along the hill.

Oh, and that wasn't the worst of it. A nice wind was coming his way too. The hot gusts of a sirocco.

Heat blasted his face like a furnace. His eyes teared up, and he blinked. Another blast of wind—this time sand got in his face. Wonderful.

"God!" His voice trembled with rage. "Yahweh!"

Yahweh was doing this, all right. The city was still standing, and Jonah was here being scorched to death. First he got shade, then he got heat.

"Kill me now!" Jonah's voice cracked. He took a deep, ragged breath—then tried getting to his feet. He nearly fell over with another blast of heat, eyes tearing so badly he couldn't see. He stumbled, dust rising. "I'd rather die than see this city standing."

Do you have a right to be angry about the vine?

The vine? Jonah blinked, turning back to the tattered corpse of what had given him shade. He rubbed his eyes—then gasped as heat and sand blasted him. "Yes! It was a wonderful vine! It was giving me shade and didn't do anything to you!"

But do you have a right to be angry?

"I do." Jonah's lips curled. He raised a shaking fist, then put it on his chest. "I am angry enough to *die*!"

Silence. Another blast of heat swept his face, stinging his eyes.

You've been so concerned about this vine. This small plant. It sprang up overnight—it died in the same amount of time.

"Yeah." Jonah wiped sweat from his brow, licking his dry lips. It was getting even harder to swallow. "It was a nice vine."

It was only a vine. Another blast of heat. *They are quite common, you know.*

"Your point?"

Nineveh has over a hundred and twenty thousand people between the whole Decapolis. A hundred and twenty thousand! And they can't tell their right hand from their left. Not to mention all the cattle.

"Yeah, I noticed." Jonah stared at the city, teeth clenched. "I see them."

Should I not be concerned about that great city?

"They're your *enemies*!" Jonah's voice cracked. He shook his fists. "Your enemies, Yahweh!"

So were you.

Jonah blinked. He looked down, his fists loosening. "That is true."

You cried out to me in your distress, and I rescued you from the roaring waves. And wasn't seaweed wrapped around your throat?

"To the roots of the mountains I sank down." The words were a hoarse whisper in Jonah's mouth. "The earth, her bars against me."

I sent a fish to rescue you. And while inside, you were quite thankful for my mercy. What did you say again?

Jonah swallowed—and this time, the lump in his throat was much more painful. "Salvation—" his voice cracked, and he shook his head. His fists tightened again.

What did you say while inside the whale?

"What I have vowed I will make good." Jonah mumbled his next words. "Salvation comes from Yahweh."

And I give it to all whom I choose.

Jonah kept his eyes on the ground. Not like he could argue with that.

I will have mercy on whom I will have mercy, and I will have compassion on whom I will have compassion. So I ask again.

Jonah turned his eyes to the heavens. His closed his eyes, exhaling.

So should I not be concerned for all those people?

† † †

The Present

Midday at Sychar. The sun beat down on Sariah's head, and she adjusted the empty pitcher on her shoulder. Kind of a shield against Samaria's heat. But not when the sun sat square center in the sky.

Yeah, it was kind of the worst time to be doing this. But when you were the talk of the town…well, avoiding people was better. That was just the way of things.

Sariah approached the well, dust rising with her footsteps. Someone was already sitting there—kind of rare at midday.

She squinted. Was that—? No. A Jew? Really?

"Pardon me." The Jew scratched his scraggy black beard. "It's pretty hot out here. Mind giving me a drink?"

Now this made no sense. A Jew asking *her* for a drink. A *man*, even. Who did he think he was?

"Well?"

Sariah cleared her throat. "You are a Jew—and I'm a Samaritan woman."

"So?"

She lowered the pitcher so it was resting on her hip. "So doesn't your law say we're unclean? That you're defiled just by interacting with us?" She cocked her head. "How can *you* ask me for a drink?"

The stranger shrugged. "If you knew the gift of God—and who it is that's asked you for a drink—you would've asked him, and he would've given you living water."

Living water? What on earth was that? "Sir." Sariah put a hand to her forehead. "You have nothing to draw with. The well is deep. *Where* are you supposed to get this living water?"

The stranger didn't answer. But the way he studied her was…unnerving, somehow.

"Anyway, what kind of water could you possibly draw?" She put a fist on her hip, adjusting the pitcher on her other hip. "Do you think you're greater than our forefather Jacob? He's the father of the covenant made between us and Yahweh, you know."

"Right. And everyone who drinks the water from *his* well gets thirsty again." The Jew patted the well's edge. "Otherwise you wouldn't have to keep coming back here day after day, drawing water for yourself."

"Yeah. So?"

"So whoever drinks the water *I* give him," the stranger raised his finger, then indicated himself, "will *never* thirst. Indeed, the water I give him will become in him a spring of water—welling up to eternal life!"

This man was either crazy or amazing. But he didn't seem crazy. And Sariah had nothing to lose by asking him...why not, right? "Sir. Could you maybe give me this water? I don't want to keep coming back here to draw liquid."

"Alright." Was that a smile tugging at his lips? "Call your husband and come back here."

Warmth crept into Sariah's cheeks. She pressed the pitcher against her hip, averting her eyes. "I—well, I don't really have a husband."

"You're right. You don't."

Sariah focused on him. "What?"

"In fact," the Jew raised his finger, "you've had five husbands. The guy you're currently shacked up with isn't one of them. So yeah, I'd say you've told me the truth."

Her jaw dropped. This man *knew* things! How was that possible?

"Sir." Sariah cleared her throat. "You're a prophet. I can tell. You could probably tell me my life story."

The stranger just stared at her, leaning forward so his elbows were on his knees. One eyebrow rose. "And?"

"I need to know—since you have knowledge from Yahweh—look." She swallowed, licking her lips. "Our fathers worshiped on this mountain. Right?" She pointed in the distance, as if the Jew could see it. "But you Jews claim that the place where we have to worship is in Jerusalem. That Temple of yours."

Now the man grinned outright. "Believe me, woman." He chuckled. "A time is coming when you won't worship the Father on this mountain *or* Jerusalem."

Sariah gasped. "What?"

"You Samaritans worship what you don't know. We Jews worship what we do know. After all," he spread his hands, "salvation comes from the Jews."

And there it was. That old Jewish superiority. Sariah tried not to roll her eyes.

"Yet—" the Jew raised his finger, "—a time is coming, and has now come, when the *true* worshipers will worship the Father in Spirit and Truth. Not in the mountain or the Temple."

"Spirit and truth." This man loved to speak in riddles. Sariah threw up her free hand. "What does that even mean?"

"Those are the kinds of worshipers the Father seeks. God is spirit. Therefore, his worshipers must worship in Spirit and in Truth."

"God is spirit. Okay." That much was obvious. Sariah scratched her chin. "But what about truth? We can't worship in that unless we know things."

The stranger gave a small nod. "And?"

"And..." She gave a small sigh. Would he understand as a Jew? "You have a long line of prophets. They explain a lot to you. But we Samaritans believe in only one prophet— Moses—and the Prophet he spoke of who would come after him. For us, that's the guy who will explain everything. The Messiah."

"And that's how you will find truth. The Messiah—that is, the Christ." The Jew straightened, inhaling deeply. "I who speak to you am he."

Sariah's lips parted. What? This man was either insane or...no. She swallowed. Was he telling the truth? The things he knew...

The man's smile did not waver. "So? Do you believe?"

✝ ✝ ✝

Circa 760 BC

Sheep bleated on the hillside, grass crunching beneath their feet. Ointment glistened on their snouts, keeping the buzzing flies away. Some were tugging at clumps of grass, while others milled beside a sycamore-fig tree.

Amos sat on the hill, shepherd's staff in hand, a breeze ruffling his gray-flecked beard. His eyes were pointed north—to the Kingdom of Israel.

The land cannot bear all his words.

Amaziah—the priest of Bethel. His complaint echoed in Amos's head.

Get out, you seer!

But Amos hadn't finished his prophecy. God had sent him to the northern kingdom of Israel. Was he to abandon his flock?

Go back to the land of Judah.

Yahweh wouldn't. Yahweh abandoned no one.

Earn your bread there—and do your prophesying there. Don't prophesy any more at Bethel, because this is the king's sanctuary and the temple of his kingdom.

As if Yahweh prophesied where men desired him. The priest of Bethel had a few things to learn. It was *God's* sanctuary and the temple of *God's* kingdom. All of Israel belonged to God. But King Jeroboam would not listen.

Amos exhaled softly. And so here he was, tending his flock down in Judah. Exiled back to his homeland. Ignored and forgotten.

He poked at the grass with his staff, inhaling deeply. Truth be told, Judah wouldn't listen to him either.

Footsteps crunched the dirt. Amos focused on the road coming down from Israel.

A man was hiking along it—dark hair, clean-shaven. He had a traveler's sack over one shoulder, and his eyes were on the ground. Each step was taken carefully, as if he wasn't sure of the terrain. No doubt a northerner. The hills of Ephraim could be treacherous.

Amos opened his mouth—then stopped. He turned back to the sheep. No point prophesying to the Israelites anymore, was there?

The lion has roared—who will not tremble?

His own words. Or rather, Yahweh's—spoken through him. Amos tightened his grip on the staff, knuckles white.

The sovereign Lord has spoken—who can but prophesy?

The footsteps drew nearer. Grass crunched as the traveler left the road. Now he was coming up the hill to Amos himself. The stranger looked up at him. "Are you the one they call Amos?"

Amos arched an eyebrow. "Indeed I am. Who's asking?"

"Just a fellow prophet. Name's Jonah."

Jonah—that sounded familiar. "From Gath Hepher?"

"The son of Amittai. That's me."

Amos squinted at him. "Weren't you the one who prophesied that King Jeroboam would extend his territory from Lebo Hamath to the Sea of the Arabah?"

"Sure did." Jonah came up beside him, setting his sack down. "Mind if I take a seat?"

Amos rolled his eyes. "Fine."

"'Fine'?" Jonah set himself in the grass beside Amos. "Not too happy to see me, eh?"

"You're one of Israel's 'yes-men' prophets." Amos nudged a clump of grass with his staff. "'Prophets' like you say whatever the king wants. The nonsense that escapes your lips is no better than drool."

"But God did extend Israel's territory."

"Well, of course you have to be right about *something* now and then." Amos pulled up his knees, then set one arm across them. "Otherwise the king wouldn't keep you around, now would he?"

"Eh, I'm a patriot." Jonah shrugged. "But I've never prophesied anything false."

Amos's eyebrows went up. "Oh? And does King Jeroboam have the blessing of Yahweh?"

"I—" Jonah licked his lips, blinking. "Not exactly. And that—I've actually been thinking about a few things recently."

"Such as?"

"Well—" Jonah moved his hands in circles, as if they could help him explain. "Who exactly *are* God's enemies? It seems to me that, from the words of prophets like you, King Jeroboam—a pure-blood Israelite—fits that bill."

Amos gave a sharp nod. "That is correct."

"But others, like the Ninev—" Jonah licked his lips again, turning away. "Nevermind. I probably shouldn't even be talking to you."

This was peculiar behavior. "You've journeyed all the way from the northern kingdom. Was it simply to see me— or do you have another errand?"

"No, it was—it was to see you." Jonah put his palms on his legs, chest rising as he took a deep breath. "I heard you've said some tough things about Israel. That you've been kicked out for it. Amaziah was furious at you."

Amos closed his eyes. "That is what happened."

"And that made me think, maybe you—well, maybe you could give me an honest answer. Since you speak the truth— even when it hurts."

Amos gave a small sigh, hefting his staff. "That's me."

"So I was wondering—why do you treat the northern kingdom like God's enemies? We're born of Jacob like you. Yahweh is in covenant with us as well."

"But," Amos raised his finger, "that only worsens the problem."

"What do you mean?"

"As God declared through me—back when Israel was at least pretending to listen—'You only have I chosen of all the families of the earth. Therefore'—" he enunciated his next words, "—yes, '*therefore*, I will punish you for all your sins.'"

"So our covenant with God is the *basis* of his judgment on us?" Jonah scratched his chin, looking off at the clouds. "Interesting."

"Most Israelites think the covenant gives them a pass to do evil. As long as they make sacrifices, it's fine—right?" Amos waved dismissively. "Alright then—go to Bethel and sin! Go to Gilgal and sin some more! Tell the priests, 'Confession time—here's what I did this week.' Then say ten prayers to Yahweh, burn a couple goats and do everything all over again *next* week!" Amos's lips curled. "But God cares. You understand? He gave Israel empty stomachs, withheld rain from them, struck their gardens and vineyards, sent plagues among them—filled their nostrils with the stench of their own casualties in war—even overthrew some of them. Just like Sodom and Gomorrah."

"I've noticed." Jonah swallowed. "He has all but set us aflame."

"He would have—but I begged him not to because you are too small, and he took pity on you." Amos inhaled deeply, focusing on the sheep. "You were like a burning stick snatched from the fire. You know that? All of you."

Jonah bit his lip. He nodded silently, eyes on the pasture. "M-hm."

What was Jonah thinking? Amos turned to him, his brow furrowing. "You really know that, Jonah?"

Jonah's lips barely parted. "Salvation comes from Yahweh."

"That's right. Seek good—not evil—that you may live." Amos held up his finger. "*Then* Yahweh Adonai of Hosts will be with you—just as you say he is."

Jonah leaned forward, shoulders hunched. He plucked a piece of grass, shaking his head. "Is Israel doomed then? We cannot keep his commands."

Amos's eyebrows went up. "Interesting that you should ask that."

"Why?"

"My latest vision. The last one I'll have, I think. I saw the Lord standing by the altar. He gave me an astounding vision of the future."

Jonah glanced at him. "What did he say about Israel?"

"That you'll be exiled."

Jonah nodded—probably more to himself than Amos. "M-hm."

"But that's not the end of the story. God says, 'For I will give the command, and I will shake the house of Israel among all the nations as grain is shaken in a sieve,'" Amos pretended he was gripping an invisible sieve, "'and not a pebble will reach the ground.'"

"Not a pebble? What does that mean?"

"God goes on to say, 'All the sinners among my people will die by the sword, all those who say, "disaster will not overtake or meet us."'" Amos jabbed his finger at the ground. "But not a single *pebble*. Those who are called by God's name will return."

Jonah nodded. "And I suppose that would include the Gentiles?"

"Apparently." Amos held up a hand to keep Jonah from interrupting. "I know. You might think me crazy. But I know who spoke to me—and Yahweh's words are always true. He says, 'In that day I will restore David's fallen booth. I will repair its broken pieces, restore its ruins, and build it as it used to be—'"

"So there will be restoration—"

"'So that—'" Amos cast him a warning glance, "'*So that* they may possess the remnant of Edom—and all the nations that bear my name.'"

Jonah jerked upright. "All the—what?—All the *nations* that bear God's name? Plural?"

"That's what he said. And it makes sense." Amos held up his hand again. "Listen, Jonah. God's promise to Abraham was that all nations would be blessed through him. And the word I used for possession here—possessing the remnant of Edom and all the nations that bear God's name—it's no coincidence that it's the same one used in the Law to describe Joseph making his grandsons Ephraim and Manasseh into sons. They are part of the tribes of Israel today because Joseph possessed them."

"So the—the nations that 'bear God's name'—they'll become part of God's people?" Jonah shook his head. "No. I can't. This is—"

"God's plan." Amos scratched his beard, leaning back. "And there's little you can do about it, Jonah. Yahweh loves even the remnant of Edom."

"But Edom is—" Jonah gave a sardonic chuckle, "Amos, you can't really believe that. Edom is the nation descended from Jacob's brother Esau. They're supposed to be our brother, but they raid and pillage us!"

"Your point?"

"When we say 'Edom,' we use that horrible nation to represent the stubbornness of the world—the part that rebels against Yahweh."

"And sometimes, Israel falls under that category." Amos hefted his staff. "But as the wise woman of Tekoa told Joab, God devises ways so that those banished from his presence will not remain estranged from him."

Jonah closed his mouth. He put a finger to his lips, eyes narrowed. "He does that."

"Perhaps you have never experienced that in your own life."

Jonah gave a small chuckle. "Oh, I definitely have."

"Have you?"

"I, uh—well, a lot of things have happened lately. Things that have…made me question my outlook on the nations and God's plan for the world."

"In what ways?"

"Well, those people who bear God's name—who will become part of God's people..." Jonah licked his lips, closing one hand into a fist. "I've had some interactions with a few of them."

Amos arched an eyebrow. "And?"

"And..." Jonah looked up at the sky, his lips pressed together. Clearly the prophet was struggling with something. "And I think I need to write it down."

Amos nodded. "That's a great idea. I'll do the same with my own prophecies."

"It wouldn't be unprecedented. I've heard other prophets in other nations are doing the same."

"Indeed." Amos inhaled deeply, gazing off at the clouds. "And people need to know. For the future's sake, if nothing else."

Jonah nodded in return, a smile tugging at his lips. "If nothing else."

"He who forms the mountains, creates the wind," Amos clutched at the air with his free hand, "and reveals his thoughts to man."

Jonah looked at him, his hands on the grass.

"He who turns dawn to darkness, and treads the high places of the earth." Amos closed his eyes—and he whispered the last words. "Yahweh of Hosts is his name."

✝ ✝ ✝

The Present

"Guys!" Sariah beckoned wildly with one hand, eyes wide. She was practically squealing. "Guys, you've got to come to the well! This guy is amazing!"

People were already approaching her. Some were curious—others probably just wanted to humor her so she would shut up.

"I'm serious! He told me everything I ever did! And he's a Jew—but he spoke to me! He reached out to *me*!"

And *that* was the kicker. Anyone talking to Sariah had to be ignorant. After the things she'd done—the men she'd slept with…

But this Jew…he was different. He knew everything—and he'd spoken to her anyway.

Sariah grinned. People were walking past her, heading for the well. They would discover him too. She couldn't wait!

She gave a small leap of joy, shaking the jug. "He's the Savior of the world!"

† † †

Early 7th Century BC

"And now the Lord says—" Isaiah paused, studying his audience. They all leaned forward with wide eyes, mouths open. A smile tugged at his lips. "'He who formed me in the womb to be his servant—to bring Jacob back to him and gather Israel to himself.'" Isaiah grabbed at the air with one hand. He waved his staff in the other. "'For I am honored in the eyes of the Lord—and my God has been my strength.'"

No one moved. This was a song of the Servant of Yahweh—the Messiah! No wonder they were holding their breath.

Isaiah cleared his throat. "He says, 'It is too small a thing for you to be my servant to restore the tribes of Jacob and bring back those of Israel I have kept.'"

Too small? He could see confusion flashing across their faces. How could the restoration of Israel be too small?

"'I will also make you a light for the Gentiles,'" Isaiah raised his finger as people gasped, "'that you may bring my salvation...'" He raised his eyes heavenward, lifting his staff. "'To the ends of the earth.'"

04 • A PROPHET WITHOUT HONOR

LUKE 5:1-11

Eighteen years earlier

"Jesus! His name is Jesus!" Joseph clutched the merchant's shoulder. "Have you seen him?"

The merchant threw up his hands and shook his head. No Jesus here.

"He's just a boy," Joseph added, pleading with his hands. "Surely—hey you! Have you seen my child?" He motioned for the attention of a passing family. "He's about this high—"

"No one has seen your son," a man snapped. "And no one is going to. Have you seen the streets of Jerusalem? He's probably lost." He shook his head as he walked away. "You'll never find him. Not in a million years."

"How did you lose him?"

Joseph turned to find an old lady with a basket. She narrowed her eyes at him. "And why did you let him out of your sight?"

Joseph sighed. "We went back to Nazareth in caravans," he explained, his words running together, "I thought he was with Mary, Mary thought he was with me—"

"How old is he?"

"Only twelve."

The old lady's eyebrows went up. "Oh…about a man now, is he?"

Joseph gave a half-hearted smile. "Yes, that's right. Have you seen any boys without their parents?"

The woman shook her head. "Not that I recall," she said slowly. "They sure grow quickly, don't they?"

"Two days ago," Joseph said. "We left from the feast of the Passover two days ago and travelled for a day, then travelled back yesterday."

The old lady nodded. "And I'll be sure to tell you if I see one."

"Thank you."

"Does he have brown eyes? My son has brown eyes too…"

"Mother!" A man ran to the old lady, wrapping his arms around her. "I'm so glad I found you." He nodded apologetically to Joseph. "I hope she hasn't troubled you."

Joseph shook his head with a jerk. "Mm-m."

"Look at that. So kind." A smile crinkled the woman's face. "I hope you find that child of yours."

"So do I."

"Joseph." A tap on his shoulder. He turned to find a black-haired woman with tears in her eyes. "Joseph, have you…" she looked around him and stopped. No Jesus.

"Still looking," Joseph said softly, putting his arm on her shoulder. "Nothing yet."

Mary looked at the sky desperately, teeth clenched. "One day," she said, voice trembling. "One day and he's gone."

"Shh." Joseph drew her close. "We'll find him. He's here." He closed his eyes. "He has to be here."

✝ ✝ ✝

"The Spirit of the Sovereign Lord is upon me, because the Lord has anointed me to preach good news to the poor." The rabbi held out the scroll of Isaiah. "He has sent me...

"To bind up the brokenhearted,

"To proclaim freedom for the captives,

"And release from darkness for the prisoners,

"To proclaim the year of the Lord's favor," he paused to take a breath, "and the day of vengeance of our God."

> *"To comfort all who mourn," the prophet Isaiah continued, patting the shoulder of a nearby widow, "and provide for those who grieve in Zion." He moved slowly toward a man in the crowd, leaning on his staff. "To bestow on them a crown of beauty," he stretched his fingers above the man's head, "instead of ashes." He made a pouring motion with steady fingers over a child's head. "The oil of gladness instead of mourning." Now he indicated himself, letting his hand run down his robe. "And a garment of praise instead of a spirit of despair."*

With a deep breath, the rabbi lowered the scroll. "Today, we are discussing the words of the Prophet Isaiah regarding the coming of our Messiah." He strolled along the circle of teachers and students sitting on the ground, then sat in the first gap he came to. "Any thoughts?"

"I have a question—for the students." A rabbi turned to some of their pupils in the circle. "Which of you can tell me why Isaiah is speaking as though he is the Messiah?"

One student raised his hand. "He speaks by the Spirit of *YHWH*," he said brightly, "So sometimes he speaks as if he is *YHWH*, sometimes as if he is Isaiah, and sometimes—like now—as if he is our Messiah."

The rabbi nodded briefly. "And how can we tell that he is speaking like the Messiah?"

Another student raised his hand. "Rabbi Simeon says he has been anointed to proclaim the year of the Lord's favor," he said eagerly, "When the Messiah releases captives and rescues us all from our enemies—and rules over the whole world as king."

Now a smile wrinkled the rabbi's face. "The day of vengeance," he said, nodding. "An astute insight, Eleazer." He pointed to another student whose hand was raised. "Yes, Jesus?"

"Rabbi Samuel, are the day of vengeance and the year of the Lord's favor the same?"

The rabbi blinked. "Excuse me?"

The boy held out his palm, and a rabbi handed him the scroll. "Well, it looks like he's talking about two different times."

Now the rabbi's eyebrows creased. "What makes you say this?"

"Well look," Jesus pointed at a few lines in the scroll. "He says he will preach good news to the poor. Is that something you do during war?"

"But his news will be that of freeing captives and releasing prisoners," Rabbi Samuel observed. "That's a very war-specific action, don't you agree?" He indicated another rabbi. "After all, if Rabbi Matthias or I tried to free captives from a Roman cell, we would have to bring an army!"

Some of the students laughed. There were a few chuckles from the other rabbis.

The boy shrugged. "Sin is captivity," he said seriously. "As the psalmist writes, 'Set me free from my prison,' and Jeremiah says, 'Your wrongdoings have kept these away;

your sins have deprived you of good.'" He tilted his head as the other students whispered to each other. "War comes in many forms."

Rabbi Samuel raised his eyebrows and looked around. "Those passages do deal with sin," he said patiently. He leaned back and stroked his beard. "What causes you to read the Isaiah passage in this way?"

"Well," Jesus took a deep breath, "he says he's going to bind up the brokenhearted." Now he surveyed the students. "People bind up wounds in war, right?"

Some of the students nodded—but others looked to the rabbis for direction.

"Now think about it." Jesus focused on Eleazer. "In what kind of war would those wounds be spiritual?"

Eleazer looked from Rabbi Samuel to Jesus, uncertain. He swallowed and, scratching the back of his neck, answered, "A war for their hearts."

Now the whispering among the students increased, and some of the rabbis began murmuring to each other. What was the boy saying?

Rabbi Samuel cleared his throat. "And do you think the Messiah will come in vengeance to judge the world?"

"Absolutely," the boy nodded, "in his own timing, of course." Then he pointed at the rabbi's heart. "But he must set you free from this prison first."

Another rabbi joined the conversation. "So why not do both at the same time?" he asked patiently, spreading his hands. "Why come twice when he can do it all at once?"

Jesus thought for a moment. "He wants to release more prisoners."

† † †

"Pardon me. Have you—have you seen our son?" Mary pleaded with a passing Pharisee. "His name is Jesus."

The Pharisee scrutinized her for a moment. "There is a child by that name who has been at the Temple for the past two days now…this will be his third day."

"May we see him?"

The Pharisee considered. "No parents have claimed him." He turned and beckoned for her to follow. "Perhaps he is yours."

"Joseph!" Mary shouted to her husband, who was speaking with another merchant. "Joseph, come quickly!"

He turned and ran toward her, watching the Pharisee with a question in his eyes.

"He thinks our son might be in the Temple," she whispered quickly.

Joseph looped his arm around Mary's. "We'll see," he said quietly. Now they kept pace with the Pharisee. "We've looked everywhere else."

✝ ✝ ✝

"Well, Jesus, your insights are interesting." Rabbi Samuel smiled gently. "Even if they lack academic value on certain points."

Jesus dipped his head. "Thank you, rabbi."

"I wonder," Rabbi Matthias took a deep breath, "what do you think of the Messiah's origin? Did he exist before creation—or is he a descendant of David?"

"The Prophets say both," Jesus answered immediately, "as the Prophet Micah says, 'whose origins will be from of old, from ancient times'—and he says that in the same breath as the declaration that the Messiah will come from Bethlehem."

A few of the rabbis nodded to each other, while others shook their heads. Rabbi Matthias arched an eyebrow, turning to Rabbi Samuel. "You doubt this boy's words, my friend?"

Rabbi Samuel graciously wagged his finger. "How can the Messiah come before David if he is his descendant?"

Jesus turned his attention to Rabbi Samuel. "May I ask you a question, Rabbi?"

Rabbi Samuel narrowed his eyes at his friend, then turned to Jesus. "You may ask all of us," he answered, spreading his arms. "That is why we are here."

"What do you think the Mountain of the Lord is?"

Some of the rabbis muttered surprise. This boy had an excellent knowledge of the Scriptures. "The Prophet Micah and the Prophet Isaiah were referring to the reestablishment of the Davidic kingship," one of them answered, gesturing. "To the days when the Messiah would rule over the Earth and Israel's prosperity would be restored."

The boy scrutinized him. "So what about the wolf and the lamb lying next to each other—and the lion eating straw like an ox? Can that really happen in our world?" He shook his head. "Conquering earthly kingdoms would not be enough to change a lion's nature."

Another rabbi leaned in. "What are you suggesting? That this will occur in the afterlife?" He waved a hand dismissively. "Do you think the Messiah will delay so long?"

"I know the Messiah will not delay." Jesus considered, pressing his lips together. "But his eternal dominion over all creation—*that* will come later."

"So what are his plans then?" Rabbi Samuel asked. "Bind up broken hearts and leave—promising to return with retribution?"

Jesus shook his head. "He's planning to save the world."

"Jesus!"

Jesus's parents stood in the doorway with a Pharisee. "Jesus, praise God!" Mary ran to Jesus, taking him in her arms. "Oh, we were so worried..." She leaned back and looked him in the eyes. "Why have you treated us like this?" A tear slid down her cheek, and she pointed to Joseph. "Your father and I have been *anxiously* searching for you."

"Why were you searching for me?" Puzzlement crept over Jesus' face. "Didn't you know I had to be in my Father's house?"

There were snickers among the students, who quieted when Rabbi Matthias raised a finger to his lips.

Mary pulled him close and kissed the top of his head. She sighed and rested her chin on his shoulder. "I'm just glad we found you."

Jesus smiled. "I've been here all along."

"Your son is very insightful," Rabbi Samuel observed, standing up. He nodded toward Joseph. "You should be proud."

Joseph smiled. "Thank you, Rabbi," he said, raising an eyebrow. "He has always been invested in Scripture." He came up behind Mary, patting her on the shoulder. "Let's go," he whispered. "We have a long journey ahead—and we're way behind schedule."

Mary nodded, sniffing. She stood up, taking Jesus's hand with a smile. Then she focused on the rabbis. "Thank you so much."

The Rabbi acknowledged her gratitude with a nod. "Take care of him." He pointed at Jesus. "That one has great potential."

Mary turned to Joseph. Her husband smiled, and the family made their way to the exit. The boy glanced back one last time—then they crossed the threshold, and the rabbis were out of sight.

† † †

Almost twenty years later

Midmorning at Nazareth. Small town, not much activity. People washing clothes, chatting idly—laughing, working, arguing. Nothing new here.

A man entered the town. Dust rose with each step.

Some people by the entrance noticed and looked up. They stopped talking and stared. A few more people in the street turned as the man made his way toward them.

"Isn't that Jesus?"

Whispers began. Jesus! The carpenter's son. Wasn't he a preacher now?

"What's he doing back?"

"Has he come to preach at us?"

"I heard he performed some miracles over in Cana."

"Oh yeah, he's famous now."

The preacher moved down the street, nodding congenially to everyone. A few nodded back, but most were wary.

More whispers.

† † †

"Mom! Guess who's here!"

Mary folded another tunic and looked up. Simon stood in the doorway grinning. She almost smiled in return. "I don't like guessing."

"It's Jesus!"

Jesus? Mary's mouth dropped. He was back! She folded the last tunic, set the clothes aside and turned to Simon. "How long ago did he arrive?"

"About ten minutes." Simon cocked his head. "Are you coming?"

As if she would say no. "I'll be there."

"Okay." Simon ran off calling, "James! Joses! Jude!"

Mary moved slowly to the entrance of their house. She watched the courtyard, waiting for her son to come home.

† † †

"So he's back in town." James smiled sardonically. "About time."

Simon's eyebrows went up. "Are you coming or not? He is our brother."

James tightened his jaw. "I suppose that's true."

"Good!" Simon pointed across the courtyard. "Joses and Jude are coming too!"

† † †

Jude gazed across the courtyard. "It's been six months," he whispered, arms crossed. "And what has he been doing in the meantime? Preaching?"

"He's been performing some miracles too." Joses shrugged. "I mean, what if he's a real prophet?"

"Uh, no. He's our brother." Jude shook his head, frowning. "He will *always* be our brother, Joses."

"I know. But—"

"But what?" Jude threw up his hands. "Unless I hear a good intellectual argument, I will never see him as anything more."

Footsteps in the courtyard. The brothers turned to see Jesus entering. The supposed prophet waved with a smile.

"Jesus!" Simon ran to greet him. "Man, we've missed you!"

Jesus hugged his younger brother, then turned and shook Joses' hand. Jude nodded curtly at him, and Jesus returned the nod affectionately. James came up from behind and patted him on the shoulder, and Jesus turned to him. "James! Good to see you."

"You too." James averted his eyes. "It's been a while."

"Yes, James, it has." Jesus kept his eyes on him. "But I have not forgotten you."

James stared at him for a moment—then indicated the house with his head. "Mother is waiting."

"I know." Jesus stepped toward the house, and James beckoned for his brothers to follow.

From the threshold Mary smiled, then retreated through the doorway.

✝   ✝   ✝

"So Jesus, what've you been up to?"

Jesus tossed some dry grass into the oven. "Well, Simon, I've been preaching that the kingship of God is near—which I call the kingdom of God."

"What do you mean? Like the Messiah?"

"Yep." Jesus briefly checked the fire in their oven. "The day of the Lord's favor—just as the prophets spoke of it— but with the day of vengeance still ahead."

"Have you done any more miracles?"

"Oh yes." Jesus tossed more grass in, chuckling. "People won't leave me alone—even when I need to sleep. They want miracles."

"What kinds?"

"Well..." Jesus checked the oven again. "I've cast out demons, healed people—"

James broke into the conversation. "What kind of people?"

Jesus and Simon focused on James, who was fixing a table. James set one of the legs down, enunciating his next words. "What kind of people did you heal?"

"Well, anyone who had faith," Jesus answered. "Men, women, children, paralytics, lepers, the lame, the deaf— even an official's son."

James narrowed his eyes. "Did the official pay you any money for healing his son?"

"No. And I wouldn't have taken any." Jesus patted Simon's arm. "Could you get me some leeks and onions from the storeroom?" As his brother ran off he added, "And bring some lentils while you're at it."

He turned back to James. "You know I have no favoritism."

James nodded, then returned to his work. "Good," he said firmly, "see that it stays that way."

Jesus nodded in return. "It will." He glanced at Mary, who was kneading the dough. "The oven is ready."

Mary pushed a strand of hair from her face. "Good," she said, handing him an unbaked piece of bread. "We can begin making the flat loaves."

Jesus accepted the bread with a smile. "Hey, you never know," he said, sticking the bread atop the oven. "We might even have this done by the time Joses and Jude return with the fish."

"Don't count on it." James switched tools. "This leg is being stubborn, so I won't be able to help anytime soon."

"Stubborn?" Jesus's brow furrowed. "Let me see that."

James sighed—then tossed him the leg. "See what you can do with it."

Jesus turned the table leg over in his hands. "How did it break?"

"Oh, you know Simon." James rolled his eyes. "He tripped when he was running in the door, and—well, we're not sure how—"

"But the table broke," Jesus finished, grinning.

"Yep." James shook his head. "Some people never grow up."

Jesus' smile faded. "And some people grew up too quickly."

"I'm back!"

Jesus turned to find Simon holding lentils, leeks and onions. "Great! See what else mom wants help with. And James…" Jesus shrugged. "Don't worry about the table. We'll work on it later."

James gave a sharp nod, setting his tools down. "Agreed."

The meal would begin any moment. The brothers were setting the table—propped on an unsteady leg—while Mary and Jesus washed a few cups outside. Simon collected two cups and ran back into the house.

"He grows more every day." Jesus grinned. "Soon he'll be a carpenter."

"M-hm." Mary glanced at the doorway. "He's almost a man."

"Is he getting married?"

She shook her head. "Not yet," she answered, scrubbing a cup. "But we're looking into it."

"Of course."

"And what about you? What are your plans in life?"

Jesus inhaled deeply, accepting a cup from her. "That is not for me to decide. I can only do what the Father tells me to."

Mary studied him. There was a sadness in her eyes, and she reached for another cup without looking at it. "That is your mission," she said softly, rewetting the cloth, "isn't it?"

"Mom…" Jesus put a hand on her arm. "I know you were hesitant to see me leave—"

"You began your true job." Mary finished wiping the cup's edges. She handed it to Jesus and averted her eyes. "I knew it had to be done—you're the Messiah, after all. But you're also my son."

Jesus put a hand on her shoulder. "I know what you fear," he whispered, setting his cup aside. "But these things *must* happen for everything to be fulfilled."

"Everything?" Mary swallowed, then reached for another cup. "I can't accept that." She shook her head. "What am I to do with you? I know you have a mission, a duty to your heavenly Father, a people to save, but—" tears welled in her eyes, "—isn't there another way? Can't you just march in and liberate us now?"

"No." Jesus squeezed her shoulder. "But this way is best."

"And how do you feel about it?"

Jesus considered, fingers tightening around his cup. "It is a difficult road," he hesitated, lips parted. His next words were barely a whisper. "But it must be done."

"But how do you *feel*?"

Jesus did not answer. He gazed into the beginnings of the sunset and swallowed. "I'm conflicted," he whispered. "I know what I must do, and I will do it." He took a deep breath. "But a great part of me wishes it did not have to be this way."

Mary scrubbed out the inside of her cup and handed it to him. "You've always been able to do that, you know." She shook her head, tears in her eyes. "Even when you were young. But now—" she kept her eyes on the last cup, voice unsteady, "now I fear—" her eyes dropped to the ground.

Jesus finished drying the cup. "You cannot change the future, mom."

"I know." A tear slid down her cheek. "But what if they kill you?" She lowered her voice. "What if they beat you? And torture you, and—" she closed her eyes, lips pressed together. "I don't know if I can handle that."

Jesus studied her. Then he reached over and took the last cup from her. He dried it in silence, keeping his eyes on the cup.

"Thank you." She replaced the wet cloth with shaking hands. Then she took a deep breath and, swallowing, asked, "Do you know where Simon went?"

Jesus shrugged. "I suppose he got sidetracked." He grabbed the four cups and handed her two. "But we can take these ourselves."

Mary gave a half-hearted smile. "Always a servant."

Jesus looked into her eyes. "And still your son."

† † †

Another day at Nazareth. People at work, children playing, and two sweaty men in a courtyard, fixing a table.

"What exactly happened?"

"No one knows except Simon." James shook his head, a smile tugging at his lips. "And Simon never knows."

Jesus chuckled. "Well," he began, grunting as he lifted the table on its side, "he didn't harm it too badly. It's just that leg he knocked out."

"He was careless." James propped their table on the bench. "He always is."

"He'll grow." Jesus picked up the table leg. "How has the trade been?"

James considered. "As good as can be expected," he answered, measuring the corner. "Can't complain."

Jesus nodded. "And how are you?"

"Good." James hesitated, eyes on the table. "Listen, brother." He grabbed a tool from the workbench. "I respect your work—as a carpenter. Especially after father died." He clenched his jaw. "Why did you leave?"

"Because my father told me to."

"Your heavenly Father."

"M-hm." Jesus bent down and measured the table leg next to the corner. "I can do only what my Father commands."

James pursed his lips, breathing in through his nose. "Right. You're serious about this, aren't you?"

"Absolutely." Jesus test-fitted the leg, then focused on his brother. "You know, my job now isn't too different from carpentry. I'm still fixing things."

"As a preacher?"

"Well, for a time, I built and rebuilt furniture. Now, my job is to build and rebuild lives." He arched an eyebrow. "And I'm more than a preacher."

James scoffed. "I can't believe you're a prophet," he spat, removing a broken dowel from the table corner. "It's too much, Jesus. Even for you."

"And what would make you believe?"

"It's not what you say that matters to me." James stared at him, eyes burning. "It's what you do."

Jesus nodded. "Fair enough."

James inserted the dowel peg. "That should hold it."

"Let's try it out."

James held the table steady while Jesus inserted the leg. Jesus twisted the leg, fit it into the dowel—then stepped back and wiped his brow.

"Looks perfect," James said, standing up. "Good work."

"M-hm. Let's get it inside." Jesus picked up one end while James grabbed the other. "I'm glad we got it done before Sabbath."

James expelled a breath as they moved into the house. "Yep."

"James." They set the table down, and Jesus's eyebrows rose. "You *will* see action."

"Will I?"

"You bet." Jesus put his hand on James's shoulder—then squeezed it. "The kingdom of God is near, brother."

† † †

10th Century BC

"I will give you thanks, for you answered me." The musician plucked a string on his lyre. "You have become my salvation."

Tables stretched under the massive tent, Israelites chewing and smacking as they devoured the Passover lamb. Cloaks tucked into their belts, one hand holding a staff—as per the Law of God.

"The stone the builders rejected has become the capstone." The musician hesitated, brow furrowing. This "stone" had entered the gates of righteousness when no one else could. Yet now it would be rejected?

He licked his lips, looking at the sky. He whispered the next words, lips barely parting. "The Lord has done this—and it is marvelous in our eyes."

✝ ✝ ✝

The Present

Sundown at Nazareth. The Sabbath had begun.

Jesus entered the synagogue with a dozen other men, moving to one side of the room while the women found their places on the other.

"Hear, O Israel." The chazzan's voice rang out over the gathering. "The Lord our God, the Lord is one." He closed his eyes, raising his hands. "Love the Lord your God with all your heart and with all your soul and with all your strength." Then he bowed his head and led the people in a prayer.

Amen.

He cleared his throat and pulled out a large scroll. "Today's reading will be from Isaiah," he said. "And since we have a very special visitor today, we are going to let him read and speak."

All faces turned to Jesus, who was sitting cross-legged by his brothers. A smile tugged at his lips—and he rose to his feet. "As you wish," he said softly. Carefully he stepped between the people and reached the chazzan, keeping his eyes on the scroll.

> *He was in the world—and though the world was made through him, the world did not recognize him.*

The attendant handed Jesus the scroll of Isaiah. Jesus unrolled it silently, the crowd watching. Seconds passed as he scanned the text. Then he nodded—and the attendant stepped back.

Jesus cleared his throat. "The Spirit of the Lord is on me, because he has anointed me to preach good news to the poor." He paused, surveying the people. "He has sent me:

"To proclaim freedom for the prisoners,

"And recovery of sight for the blind,

"To release the oppressed—" here he smiled—

"To proclaim the year of the Lord's favor." And there he stopped.

Jesus rolled up the scroll, inhaling deeply. He handed it to the attendant with a "thank you." Now came the teaching.

All eyes were fastened on the preacher. Watching—waiting for his next words.

Jesus spoke. "Today this Scripture is fulfilled in your hearing."

He came to that which was his own, but
his own did not receive him.

Whispers in the crowd.
Is he serious?
Sure, he's a wise person, but—
Messiah! Yeah right!
Isn't this Joseph's son?

Laughter. "I knew you when you were a snot-nosed child!"

"You used to play hide-and-seek with my kids when you were five!"

"So the carpenter thinks he's a prophet!"

"Oh no, much more than that! He thinks he's the Messiah!"

More laughter.

Jesus held up a finger. "Surely you will quote this proverb to me: 'Physician, heal yourself!'" The room went silent. "'Do here in your hometown all the stuff we heard you did everywhere else.'" He leaned forward. "So you want proof? You want me to perform a miracle?"

No one replied. Some exchanged glances—and others shook their heads.

"I tell you the truth." Jesus gritted his teeth. "*No* prophet is accepted in his hometown." He thrust a trembling finger at his audience. "I can assure you—oh, without a doubt— that there were many widows in Israel in Elijah's time, when the sky was shut for three and a half years and there was a severe famine throughout the land." He clutched at the air with his fingers. "Yet Elijah was not sent to any of them— any of them!—But to a widow in Zarephath," he turned to face the women, "in the region of Sidon."

The crowd gasped. Did he dare—? Was he actually saying they were as hardened as their ancestors in Elijah's time?

"And there were many in Israel with leprosy in the time of *Elisha* the prophet, Elijah's successor," Jesus turned to the men, finger raised, "yet not one of them was cleansed—only Naaman." His voice shook. "The Syrian!"

The crowd erupted. Many leapt to their feet—and some rushed at Jesus, shaking their fists. In seconds he was surrounded.

"Away with him!" Someone pushed Jesus. "He's not fit to live!"

"How dare he say such things!" Another push. "The Messiah is for Jews only!"

"That the *Gentiles* of all people would receive the blessings intended for us—" a younger man shoved Jesus toward the entrance—"It's blasphemy!"

"Kill him!"

More cries. The mob began shoving Jesus out the door.

"Stop this!" Mary came up to the edge of the crowd, looking for a way in.

The crowd exited the synagogue and, forcing Jesus ahead of it, angled for a nearby hill.

James shouted in frustration and rammed a man on the mob's edge. "Jesus!" He yelled, elbowing his way through the crowd. Jude came up on the other side.

The mob pressed on, making their way up the hill. Angry hands shoved Jesus ahead.

Joses and Simon fell behind with Mary. "Please!" She screamed. "He's my son!"

"Jesus is crazy!" James retreated from the mob, out of breath. He ran to the other side of the crowd with Jude, scouring the angry mass for an opening.

"Fool," Jude gasped. "He should be glad blood is thicker than water."

"Agreed." James punched someone, then bulled his way into the crowd. "Jesus!" Someone tried to hit him, but he knocked him out of the way.

More punches. Jude lay sprawled on the ground.

Roaring, fists flying, James lunged toward Jesus. He grunted as someone hit him, kneed his attacker—dodged an elbow—threw a punch, and looked up to see Jesus at the top of the rocky outcropping.

"No!" He shouted, diving forward.

Then everything went silent.

James got to his feet, eyes darting around the crowd. What—?

The people just stood still. Their arms fell by their sides. They stared at Jesus, who gazed into their eyes.

No one moved. No one spoke.

Jesus looked from face to face, sadness in his eyes. He swallowed, then began making his way through the reticent mob. Step by step, cloak swishing as he moved past them.

James blinked. How could this happen?

Jesus walked past one man—then another. And still they just stared. Stared like they couldn't even move. Jesus strode past a trio of younger men, whose hands were limp by their sides. A few more and he was free of the crowd—without a word, without a sound.

He'd escaped.

And now the crowd was dissipating. But James kept his eyes on his brother, mouth open. He ran after him. "Wait!"

Jesus turned around.

"Wait." James stopped before him, hand outstretched. "How—?"

"By the Spirit." A tear slid down Jesus' cheek. "By the Spirit, James." He swallowed. Then he placed his hands on his brother's shoulders. "James, one day you will believe."

James stared into his brother's eyes. There was so much feeling there—compassion mingled with fury, gentleness tempered by indignation. And still deeper was purpose.

James shook his head. "You're crazy, brother."

"Am I? Only in his hometown." Jesus released his brother's shoulders, expelled a trembling breath—and raised a finger. "Only in his hometown is a prophet without honor."

"A prophet." James narrowed his eyes. "But you say you're more than a prophet."

"Yes." Jesus nodded. "Much more."

Then Jesus turned and, stepping slowly, began making his way down the path that led out of Nazareth.

05 · FOR THE SAKE OF THE CALL

LUKE 5:1-11

Circa 860 BC

The field shimmered with waves of heat, sunlight searing his bronzed arms. Elisha staggered forward, knuckles white as he clutched his plowing equipment. His oxen moved ahead, tugging the plow and snorting. Dirt crunched with each step, mingling with the locusts' chirps.

Sweat rolled down his temple, tracing his cheek and jawline. More sweat stung his eyes, and he blinked. Beside him eleven more pairs of oxen plowed, pushed by hired men.

Grass crunched at the edge of his plantation. He squinted at the hills, trying to make out the figure standing there. Camel's hair tunic, leather belt—and that face…

Elisha's eyes widened. Was that—?

He shook his head, blinking. No. He was imagining things. The head prophet of Yahweh had no reason to visit. Elisha wiped his brow with one arm, squeezing his eyes shut.

He heard footsteps. He looked up to see the figure approaching him, a cloak hanging over one arm. The long, shaggy black beard...sunken eyes burning with a passion Elisha could only begin to understand—this was Elijah. There could be no doubt.

Elijah stopped beside Elisha. The head prophet raised his cloak, grasping it in both hands. Then—without a word—he draped it over Elisha's back.

Elisha's mouth dropped. What was this? Was Elijah really asking him?

The prophet's jaw was set. His eyes locked with Elisha's—and one thick eyebrow rose.

"I, um I—" Elisha licked sweat from his lips, averting his eyes. This changed everything. Elijah was calling him to join Yahweh's ministry! To become a prophet! How could he say no? "I need to—I need to tell my parents."

Elijah studied him. The prophet inhaled deeply, eyes narrowed.

"Let me kiss them goodbye. Get their blessing." Elisha swallowed, releasing the plow. "Then I'll come with you."

"Go back." Elijah waved as if to dismiss him. "Say goodbye. After all, what have I done to you that you should leave home without a word?"

"Thanks." Elisha yanked up the plow. Then he spun to the hired men. "Hey! Stop it!"

The other men turned to him. They noticed Elijah, and their eyebrows went up. Some exchanged glances—others wiped their brows, confused.

"You're done for the day! In fact—" a grin broke across Elisha's face, "—you'll never plow for me again."

Now the murmurs began. No doubt they thought Elisha was out of his mind. Stop plowing for him? What, would Elisha do the plowing himself?

"And hand me the equipment." Elisha pointed at the ground. "Set it right here, in front of me. At my feet."

The men pulled up their plows. Most of them wouldn't even meet his eyes as they dumped the equipment before him. He had definitely lost their respect.

No matter. He was freer than he'd ever been.

Elisha spun and sprinted toward the house, feet nearly slipping in the dirt. "Mom! Dad!" He skidded to a stop by the entrance, pebbles sliding after him. "You won't *believe* it!"

His parents looked out at him with wide eyes. "Yes?"

A part of him felt numb inside. But Elisha couldn't stop smiling. "I'm going to be a prophet!"

† † †

Flames crackled and roared, sparks flying into the night. Elisha's plowing equipment splintered and cracked in the heat, molten fragments exploding as they burned.

The oxen Elisha had been plowing with were now sitting in pieces on his plate. He plunged his fork into a slice—then brought it to his mouth. Delicious.

The people sitting at his banquet still seemed incredulous. He'd invited the entire neighborhood—and truth be told, more of them were probably here for hunger than curiosity. After all, the drought had only ended a few weeks ago.

"Eat your fill," Elisha shouted through a mouthful, raising his fork. "*I* won't be eating it. I'm training under Elijah."

"What if it doesn't work out?"

He turned to his father. Shaphat had been silent up to this point—but concern lined his face. "What will you do if the ministry doesn't feed you?"

"Yahweh will provide." Elisha leaned forward, chewing his bite. He let his eyes wander over the crowd. "He always has, and he always will."

Shaphat opened his mouth—then closed it. His eyes settled on the slaughtered oxen. "I hope so."

Elisha raised a finger, swallowing his bite. "The better question is, what am I missing if I don't?"

"Probably a life of hardship and turmoil." Shaphat poked at the meat on his plate. "If you haven't noticed, our queen isn't too fond of Yahweh's prophets."

Elisha shook his head. "Yahweh has *called* me, father. And when Yahweh calls…" He spread his hands, as if it was obvious. "None can refuse."

✝ ✝ ✝

The Present

"You want to follow me? You have to count the cost." Jesus stood in the middle of Simon's boat, holding out his fingers as if counting them. "Suppose one of you wants to build a tower. Won't he first sit down and estimate the cost? After all, if he starts laying the foundation—" Jesus chuckled, surveying the crowd, "—well, if he runs out of money, everyone will make fun of him. They'll say, 'This fellow couldn't finish what he started.' All because he didn't count the cost!"

Every eye was wide. The crowd pressed against the shore, waves lapping over their feet. Though Jesus was thirty meters out, they could hear every word. That was the way sound carried over the Sea of Galilee.

Simon was untangling his net. He'd agreed to let the preacher use his boat to speak. Jesus was a master of Scripture, after all.

"Or suppose a king is going to war against another king. Don't you think he'll sit down first—consider whether he can even stand up to the other king? What if he finds out his force is much smaller?" Jesus arched an eyebrow. "He'll be glad he counted the cost first."

Simon still wasn't sure what he thought of Jesus. Andrew had introduced them a few weeks ago—and the first thing the preacher had done was give Simon a new name.

You are Simon son of John. You will be called 'Peter.'

What an odd thing to do. Most people didn't just hand out new names. But Jesus was different.

"In the same way, any one of you—" Jesus paused, pointing at the crowd, "*any* one of you who does not give up *everything* he has cannot be my disciple."

Everything, eh? Simon arched an eyebrow. Did that include their old name?

"He who has ears to hear, let him hear."

A popular catchphrase of the preacher. Simon pulled two strands of netting loose.

"A man once told me, 'I'll follow you wherever you go.' And I told him, 'foxes have holes and birds of the air have nests, but the Son of Man doesn't even have a place to lay his head.'" Jesus pointed down. "I stay at a house every night—but my home is not here. And if you follow me, your home won't be here either."

A nomadic teacher. Simon shrugged. Some were like that.

"Another man would've followed me, but he wanted to bury his mother and father first."

Some in the crowd nodded. That seemed reasonable enough.

"I told him, 'Let the dead bury their own dead, but *you* go and proclaim the kingdom of God.'"

Gasps in the crowd. Simon's brow furrowed. To leave the dead unburied—and worst of all, a man's own parents? Burying them was his responsibility! Was 'proclaiming the kingdom of God' that important? What kind of kingdom was this?

"Another would-be follower told me, "I'll follow you— but first let me go back and get my family's blessing."

More nods in the crowd. This was shaping up to be like the account of Elisha and Elijah. That was the very thing Elisha told Elijah when he was called.

"But I told him this." Jesus raised his finger, eyes searching the crowd. He leaned forward, and the boat rocked a little. "No one who puts his hand to the plow and looks back is fit for service in the kingdom of God."

More gasps. Some covered their mouths, eyes wide.

Simon focused on the preacher. What was Jesus saying? That his call was even *more* immediate than Elijah's call to Elisha? Who did this guy think he was?

"I tell you the truth," Jesus spread his arms, "if anyone comes to me and doesn't put me first—" Jesus pointed at himself, "yes, first, before your mother, your father, your brothers and sisters—and even your own life—you cannot be my disciple."

The murmurs were growing louder. Many were shaking their heads.

"And anyone who will not carry his cross and follow me cannot—" Jesus formed a fist and slammed the boat's edge, "—*cannot* be my disciple!"

The murmurs stilled. No one was moving.

Jesus inhaled deeply, straightening. "So before you follow me—you must count the cost. Because I demand all of you."

Whew. These were bold words. This preacher was really asking to be tossed off a cliff somewhere. Sure, Simon had heard he'd cured a few sicknesses—but was that really so impressive? It's not as though the man could command the forces of Yahweh's creation.

A smile tugged at the corner of Simon's lips. Now *that* would be something.

"Alright. That's it for today. Remember, the kingdom of God is near!"

The murmuring resumed. A few in the crowd exchanged glances—but most turned around. Some lingered by the shore's edge, no doubt hoping for a miracle. But when Jesus said he was done, he was done.

"Peter."

Simon looked up. Jesus was grinning at him. "Put out into deep water. Let down the nets for a catch."

Simon's chest rose as he sighed. He dropped the pieces of netting, eyes on the boat's floor. "Master…" He licked his lips. "We've worked hard all night—and haven't caught a thing."

"And?"

Simon met Jesus's eyes. This preacher was insistent. Hard to refuse. "But because…" He hesitated, swallowing. Why not. "But because you say so, I will let down the nets."

"Good!" Jesus took a seat in the boat, setting his arms on his knees. "I'll make myself at home."

Simon shrugged, nodding to Andrew. They pulled out the oars—and began angling for the deep waters of Galilee.

✝ ✝ ✝

The nets splashed into the sea, darkening as water soaked their strands. They seemed to shimmer under the glassy surface, sinking unevenly into the blue depths. Simon and Andrew held each end of the line with both hands, sitting by the boat's edge.

Not that they expected much.

Oh look. James and John, Zebedee's sons, were coming out with them. Maybe they were tired of the empty night and were trying to catch something too.

Simon's fingers loosened on the cords. Not that you could catch anything in the middle of the day. Fish fed at night. This preacher certainly knew the Scriptures—but fishing was clearly not his thing.

Simon looked up at the sky, trying not to roll his eyes. But what could it hurt to humor Jesus? Not like they had any fish to sell today anyway.

A tug on the line.

He glanced at Andrew. His brother looked back at him, lips parting. He'd felt it too.

Another tug. Sharper than the first.

What was going on? Simon tightened his grip, gasping as the line jerked him. What was down there?

The boat began to tilt. Simon growled, muscles bulging as he tugged on the line. He and Andrew braced their feet against the boat's edge, fighting against whatever had caught in their net.

"James! John!" Simon gestured wildly, shouting. "We need you! Now!"

James and John looked over. Their eyes widened—and they began paddling fiercely, pulling up their nets with one hand.

"Grab the other side of the nets!"

James and John reached into the water, fingers curling around the netting. They tried pulling it up—but their boat only started tipping.

Simon pulled harder. He caught a glimpse of the netting—fish were wriggling furiously, packed together like bricks in a house. The creatures could barely move. He tried yanking the line again—and one cord snapped!

His mouth dropped. His eyes wandered from Andrew to James and John, but they were focused on the fish. Simon swallowed. "Pull the fish out! Dump them into the boats!"

Good thing the sons of Zebedee had brains on them. Now they were scooping the fish into their own nets—though the way both boats were tipping made Simon wonder if that was wise. The boats were sinking, like there were holes in the flooring.

But the fish kept coming. Wriggling, flopping onto their boats. More than a week's worth—

No. Simon shook his head. This was impossible. He turned his back on the fish—and his eyes met Jesus's.

The preacher was standing in the boat's center. His gaze was on Simon, lips pressed together. His brow was furrowed—but one eyebrow rose slightly.

How? This could not be a coincidence. This man—whoever he was—he'd just done the impossible. He was a miracle worker of greater clout than Simon could even fathom. Greater clout than Simon deserved to be with—

Simon thrust himself at Jesus's feet, hands splayed out and face to the boat. Fingers trembling, shaking his head. "Get away from me!"

No response. Simon pressed his face to the wood. "I am a sinful man." He swallowed, squeezing his eyes shut, fingers digging into the planks. "I don't deserve to share the same boat with you! Leave me!"

"Don't be afraid."

What? Simon's muscles loosened. "Why? I don't deserve to be near you."

"But you're a fisherman, right?"

Simon sat up, adjusting his knees on the creaking wood. Jesus was grinning at him. The preacher surveyed the other fishermen, eyes sparkling. Most of their catch was in the boats—though the bulging nets were still partly in the water. No one knew how these ships were still floating. "You're all fishermen."

"Yes." Simon swallowed. "Uneducated sinners."

"Not for much longer."

Simon's brow furrowed. "What?"

"Follow me." Jesus extended his hand, a smile tugging at his lips. "I'll make you fishers of *men*."

"What—you mean—catch people?" Peter tilted his head. Was Jesus…asking them to join him?

"That's right." Jesus nodded. "From now on you will catch men."

The other three were watching. Peter's eyes settled on Jesus's hand. What on earth would this preacher want with *him*? He was unworthy—an ignorant, dumb fisherman off the shore of Galilee.

But Jesus was asking.

"Peter."

Simon looked up at Jesus. The preacher's eyes burned with something the fisherman had never seen. "I want you to be my disciple. Be a fisher of men."

Simon's lips parted. What would drive this preacher to settle on fools like them? Simon didn't know—and part of him didn't even want to. This was so much more than the life he had. This was real.

It *meant* something.

Simon took Jesus's hand. "Peter, huh?"

Jesus grinned. "That's my name for you."

It meant "rock." Peter had been compared to one before, but never favorably. Maybe this preacher had something of the same idea. Or maybe, just maybe, Peter had no idea what Jesus was thinking.

Peter got to his feet, glancing at the other fishermen. "Well? You coming with me or not?"

Andrew nodded. "*I* am."

James and John glanced at each other. John inhaled deeply—then nodded. "What else can we do? Rabbi," he turned to Jesus, "no one is like you."

Jesus's smile did not waver. "Got that right."

✝   ✝   ✝

Waves lapped against the shore of Galilee, foaming over dead fish. A few fish still wriggled and flopped, fighting against the nets and carcasses around them. Sunlight glinted off their scales, flashing as the catch of a lifetime tried to escape.

The boats were unevenly keeled, resting on the beach with wet netting draped over their edges. Birds circled overhead—and some were already sitting on the boat's edges, heads cocked as they decided how to begin their feast.

Footprints led away from the shore, where the bluffs swallowed them. Wind swirled the grass, then died down as locusts chirped.

In the distance five figures hiked, four of them following one, their backs turned to the boats and fish.

06 • THE MISSION OF JESUS

LUKE 4:31-37

For the Son of Man came to seek and to
save that which was lost.

Dawn at Capernaum. Water lapped against the shores of Galilee. And beside a large rock, on his knees, Jesus prayed.

"Oh father," he began, eyes shut, "give me strength to do this day's work." Silently his lips moved, and he bowed his head. Then he breathed in deeply, unclasping his hands. "Thank you for this time with you."

A ray of sunlight touched his face, and he opened his eyes. Soon Capernaum would be in full swing—the markets bustling, the children playing, clothes washed, merchants haggling. Another day in Galilee.

But Jesus had work to do. He got to his feet stiffly, resting his hand on the rock. He glanced at the town—and a smile pulled at his lips.

Then, step by step, the Son of Man made his way into Capernaum—the headquarters of his ministry on this earth.

Circa 730 BC

Before King Ahaz stood Isaiah, prophet of Israel. "Nevertheless," he declared, resting on his staff, "there will be no more gloom for those who were in distress."

King Ahaz had been resting his forehead on the palm of his hand—but now he looked up. "What do you mean?"

"In the past God humbled the land of Zebulun and the land of Naphtali," Isaiah frowned. "That region was the first to suffer the wrath of Assyria."

Ahaz nodded, fists tightening. The devastation of Galilee was well known.

"But in the future he will honor Galilee of the Gentiles," Isaiah continued, "by way of the sea, along the Jordan."

"Honor them?" What a ridiculous statement. "You jest, prophet."

"The people walking in darkness have seen a great light." Isaiah's eyes rose to the palace's ceiling, and he raised his staff. "On those living in the land of the shadow of death—" he brought the staff down sharply—"a light has dawned."

Ahaz shifted in his seat. "A great light?" he asked, cautious. "You mean a deity?"

Isaiah nodded, but he kept his eyes on the ceiling. "You have enlarged the nation," he said, raising a hand. "You have enlarged the nation and increased their joy." He smiled and closed his eyes. "They rejoice before you as people rejoice at the harvest," he raised his staff victoriously, "as men rejoice when dividing the plunder."

So now Isaiah was talking to this deity. Ahaz shook his head.

"For as in the day of Midian's defeat," Isaiah continued, forming a fist, "you have shattered—shattered!—The yoke that burdens them, the bar across their shoulders—" he shook his staff, knuckles white—"the rod of their oppressor." His eyes opened, and he focused on Ahaz. "That is the light." He lowered his staff. "The hope of all Israel."

Ahaz cleared his throat. "Yes, this—eh—'Immanuel' you spoke of—this is the conquering King, right?"

Isaiah sighed. "He is much more than that," he said wearily, leaning on his staff. "His reign will bring peace—true peace. Peace with God."

The king's eyebrows creased. "But he will conquer all our enemies, right?" He leaned forward, smirking. "Assuming Yahweh has *any* power, of course. And if he's not too busy, he'll save us all and unite the nations, correct?"

Isaiah raised a hand defensively. "The peace of an eternal dominion is only superficial," he began, pointing at the King's chest, "as long as there is no peace in your heart."

"But he will conquer, right?" Now Ahaz leaned forward even more. "You said 'as in the day of Midian's defeat'—does that mean this ruler you speak of will triumph even against impossible odds?"

"Yes." Isaiah dipped his head. "But his first victory will be over the hearts of men—the greatest victory of all." He inhaled deeply, then raised his voice. "For to us a child is born, to us a son is given, and the government," he pointed at the throne, "will be on his shoulders."

King Ahaz was speechless. A child? "Really."

Isaiah stamped the ground with his staff. "And he shall be called:

"Wonderful Counselor,
Wonder of a Counselor.
"Mighty God,
The heroic God.
"Everlasting Father,
Our Father eternally.
"Prince of Peace."
The Creator of peace.

The prophet's chest heaved as he took a deep breath. "Of the increase of his government—and peace—there will be no end."

Ahaz narrowed his eyes. "How—?"

"The zeal of the Lord Almighty," Isaiah enunciated each syllable, "will accomplish this."

✝ ✝ ✝

The Present

"The time has come."

Sabbath at Capernaum. Jesus sat speaking to a crowded synagogue.

"The kingdom of God—his kingship—is near," he continued, spreading his arms. "Repent and believe the good news!"

Peter leaned in. The kingdom of God? That meant salvation for the Jews! A Messiah to save them from the Romans.

Jesus gestured at a rabbi. "And what does the kingdom of God value?"

The man considered. "Rabbi Abiathar believes that strength and wisdom will be highly valued in the kingdom."

"Wisdom is more precious than rubies." Jesus raised his eyebrows. "But what do you believe?"

The Rabbi dipped his head. "I agree with Abiathar."

Jesus turned to the others. "How about the poor?" He indicated the Rabbi. "Will they be valuable in the kingdom?"

The Rabbi shook his head. "Rabbi Ehud holds that the poor are in their situation as a result of punishment for their sins from the Almighty." He inhaled deeply. "As Rabbi Zacharias said, they are receiving what they deserve."

"No." Jesus raised an admonitory finger. "No, the poor are *very* valuable in the kingdom of God." He clutched at the air. "The kingdom of God *belongs* to the poor." His eyes sparkled as he surveyed his audience. "And the meek—they will inherit the earth!"

Gasps in the crowd. Peter blinked, running a hand through his graying hair. That was quite a bit of authority. Most teachers simply quoted other rabbis and called it good.

"Do you remember what the prophet Jeremiah says?" Jesus deepened his voice. "Let not the wise man boast of his wisdom, or the strong man boast of his strength—or the rich man boast of his riches." He motioned to the rabbi, mouth open as if he expected the teacher to continue. "But let him who boasts…"

The rabbi inhaled deeply, hands on his lap. "But let him who boasts boast about this—that he understands and knows me."

"That I am the Lord…"

"Who exercises kindness—"

"Yes!" Jesus raised his finger. "What is kindness but love to the undeserving?"

The rabbi cleared his throat. "Granted. But what of the rest of the verse?"

Jesus straightened. "That I am the Lord, who exercises kindness, justice and righteousness on earth—" his next words were a whisper, his eyes searching the audience, "for in these I delight."

No one spoke. The rabbi was rubbing his chin, studying Jesus.

"Not strength. Not riches. Not even wisdom, in one sense." Jesus made a barring motion with his hands. "Boast in the *Lord*—because knowing him is valued by him."

"Knowing Yahweh *is* wisdom," the rabbi objected.

"But not the wisdom of this world."

The rabbi scratched his chin again, averting his eyes. "I suppose…"

"Not only that, but those who weep—those who mourn, those who hunger…" Jesus pointed at a widow sitting by the opposite wall. "You are all blessed!"

Peter and Andrew exchanged glances. So the rich and strong weren't blessed—and the poor and destitute were? Was their teacher losing his mind?

"What does the psalmist say? The Lord's pleasure is not in strength, but 'in those who fear him, who put their hope in his unfailing love.'" Jesus spread his hands, grabbing at the air. "With those who are, as the Prophet Isaiah says, 'humble and contrite, and who tremble at my word.'" Now he leaned forward, lowering his voice. "With the poor in spirit."

"You can't stop me!"

The group turned as a man burst into the synagogue. His clothes were tattered, torn. He pushed a man into the wall and shouted, "I'll tear this place apart!" Then he flinched and grabbed his head. "No, no, no," he begged, speaking to himself, "no!"

He looked around, wide-eyed. He spotted Jesus—and gave a bloodcurdling scream.

Jesus stood, jaw clenched. Silently he stepped toward the possessed man.

"Ha!" The man leapt forward, spit flying from his mouth. "What do you want with us, Jesus of Nazareth?" He clutched his head once more, whimpering. "Have you come to destroy us?" He smiled suddenly. "I know who you are," he shouted, and now it almost seemed as though two voices were in his mouth. Trembling, he thrust a finger at Jesus. "The Holy One of GOD!"

"Be quiet!" Jesus said sternly.

The man twitched. He opened his mouth—but no words came out. He was choking, hissing as his eyes bulged. His fists clenched, arm muscles rippling with an unseen force.

"Come out of him!"

The man screamed, slamming onto the floor as if plunged there by an unseen hand. His body convulsed, his eyes staring into space. Then he lay still.

The man got to his knees, arms trembling as they supported him. He sputtered, blinking—then looked up at Jesus.

Jesus knelt beside him. "You are free," he said gently, taking his hand. "The demon has left you."

The people were speechless. Peter glanced at James and John—but they were just staring at their rabbi. James shook his head, mouthing "wow."

The man tried to speak—then swallowed, licking his lips. He looked into Jesus's eyes, trembling as the preacher helped him to his feet. "Thank you." His voice was barely a whisper. "I—thank you."

Jesus smiled at him. "Go in peace."

Behind him the whispers began.

Who is this man?

He has such authority! He even commands evil spirits and they leave!

And his teaching—it isn't like the teachers of the law.

No, he actually teaches as if what he says is important!

Jesus escorted the man out of the synagogue, eyes ahead. Was that Peter's cue to leave? The other three disciples turned to him, but he gave a light shrug. "Jesus is the master."

Andrew gave a small nod. "A master on a mission."

07 · Savior of the Unclean

Luke 5:12-32

2nd Millennium BC

"Unclean! Unclean!"

Eleazar the priest made his way outside the camp, sand and pebbles crunching beneath his sandals. A hot wind blew sand into his eyes, blasting his face like a furnace—and he blinked tears. Where was Abiathar?

"Unclean! Unclean!"

He glanced at the lepers to his right. Torn clothes, faces covered up to their nose. Matted hair hanging like dust weeds over grimy foreheads. Hands out as they backed away.

Eleazar swallowed, his stomach knotting. These were the unclean. No one could be with them.

"Priest! Priest, you're here!"

He nearly jumped. A leper was running toward him! Eleazar's muscles tensed—and he took a step back, mouth open. Was this—?

"I'm Abiathar! It's time for my ceremonial cleansing!"

"Yes. Abiathar." He swallowed, eyebrows rising. Of course. "Has—has your sore been healed?"

"As far as I can tell. Look—" he lifted a shred of cloth from one arm, thrusting it before Eleazar. "Look! See?"

Eleazar studied the arm. Definitely some spotted discoloration… "Seems more dullish white," he murmured, scratching his beard. "And it hasn't spread. If anything—"

"It's died down! I know!" Abiathar couldn't stop smiling. He shook the discolored arm. "I'm clean! Right?"

Eleazar glanced back at the camp. This really was the day for Abiathar's cleansing, wasn't it? Abiathar's own family knew it. He could see them at the camp's edge—one mother holding her child by the hand, waiting. Eleazar turned back to the leper, a smile curling his lips. "As soon as we perform the ritual, you're free to enter the camp where Yahweh dwells."

"Yes!" Abiathar's voice cracked. He leapt in the air, fists punching at the sky. "I'm clean!"

"Not yet." Eleazar raised his finger. "First we must get the birds."

✝ ✝ ✝

Eleazar held the live pigeon with steady fingers, one hand tight around its wings. The other hand held the ingredients of purification—hyssop, a small piece of cedar wood and scarlet yarn. He brought the bird together with the ingredients and raised them over the clay jar.

The creature spotted its reflection in the bloodied water. It tried to flap away—but Eleazar had done this many times. "Easy there," he whispered, lowering the bird.

Abiathar watched, eyes wide. His lips barely parted, his fingers splayed.

"For your cleansing," Eleazar declared, dipping the bird in the blood. He pulled out the pigeon, letting rivulets of bloodied water trickle off it. The creature shook its head, droplets flying off. "The blood of another bird was shed in this jar."

The bird shook his head again, then focused on Eleazar. It struggled against his hands—but he tightened his grip. "For your freedom," he enunciated, eyebrows rising. He focused on Abiathar. "Understand?"

Abiathar gave a sharp nod. "M-hm."

Did anyone understand? Eleazar set the ingredients down—then dipped his fingers in the jar. "Seven times." He raised his blood-tipped fingers over Abiathar's head—and sprinkled him. First time.

Abiathar closed his eyes as Eleazar dipped his fingers in again. Seven times…seven times and this part of the ritual would be complete.

Second time. Abiathar did not flinch as blood speckled his grimy forehead.

Eleazar dipped his fingers again. Third time. Ironic that touching the dead would make you unclean—but being sprinkled with blood restored your cleanliness.

Fourth time. Eleazar tried not to smile. Was it so ironic, though? After all, the life of the animal was in its blood. So really, Abiathar was being sprinkled with life.

Fifth time. Eleazar's brow furrowed. No, the true irony was how they came by that blood. By slaughtering an animal.

Sixth time. No doubt about it. In Yahweh's law, death was the only means by which life could be obtained.

The bird in his other hand was still dripping blood. Eleazar raised his fingers over Abiathar's face for the seventh time—then flicked his fingers, letting droplets of blood pelt the man's forehead. "This part is complete."

Abiathar's eyes opened. "I'm—I'm clean? I can—" he swallowed suddenly, "I can wash myself, enter—enter the camp, bring a couple lambs to sacrifice?"

"After this." Eleazar raised the dripping bird to the sky and released it. The bird fluttered into the desert, wings scattering droplets of red as it rose into the cloud-spotted canvas. The sun glinted off its feathers, and in seconds it was a speck in the sky.

Eleazar's next words were a whisper. "I pronounce you clean."

✝ ✝ ✝

22 A.D.

"The Lord said to Moses, 'Command the Israelites to send away from the camp anyone who has an infectious skin disease or a discharge of any kind, or who is ceremonially unclean because of a dead body." Rabbi Elihud held open the scroll of Bemidbar, eyes on Matthew.

Matthew bit his lip—then finished it from memory. "'Send away male and female alike—send them outside the camp so they will not defile their camp—" he inhaled deeply, "where I dwell among them.'"

"Perfect! Your memorization is flawless. And at eighteen years of age, no less."

"So it would seem." Matthew clasped his hands, folding his legs on the cushion. His eyes settled on the marble floor—and he cleared his throat.

"Yes?"

"It is just—it seems that Yahweh expels his own followers."

Rabbi Elihud's eyebrows creased. "That is a bold declaration. Yahweh welcomes all who come to him."

"Unless they're ceremonially unclean." Matthew focused on the scroll. "If they have a skin infection, have eaten something unlawful or happen to have touched something they shouldn't have, they are cut off."

"Now..." Elihud hesitated. "That is not Yahweh's fault, Matthew. It is to his credit—because he—"

"—Is perfectly holy?" Matthew's eyebrows went up. "I know, rabbi. Our God *is* perfectly holy. Far too holy for the unclean."

Elihud swallowed, rolling up the scroll. "So why complain then? God is perfect, and the unclean is burned up in his presence. It is for our safety that the unclean cannot venture near him."

"Otherwise they would be destroyed." Matthew cocked his head. "But they will all be destroyed apart from Yahweh regardless. So isn't it *really* for the sake of those in the camp who are *clean* that the unclean leave? So God doesn't destroy us all?"

"Correct. But," Elihud raised his finger, "the unclean deserve it. It is punishment for their sins."

"And can't they turn? God always welcomes those who repent."

"Yes, but..." Elihud licked his lips, eyes on the ceiling. "Matthew, some sins are simply too great. When a man has a skin disease, it is one sign of such sins. He is beyond hope."

"Beyond even the power of Yahweh?"

Anger flashed in Elihud's eyes. "It is not about what Yahweh *can* do, Matthew. It is about what he has *chosen* to do."

"Why? As he stated through the Prophet Ezekiel, he desires that none should perish."

"Yes, but that passage is a call to *repentance*. God must be just—you know this!" Elihud spread his hands, voice trembling. "He must be true to his own character—the nature of *what is good*!"

"Of course. But Yahweh could cleanse us all if he desired to."

"How?" Elihud spread his hands. "Snap his fingers? Sin is real, Matthew. No *just* God can ignore it."

"Fair enough." Matthew clenched his jaw. "So have you sinned?"

"Certainly not." Elihud raised his chin. "I have observed every command of Moses since I was a boy. I have—"

"But are you perfect?"

"Well—" Elihud gave an exasperated sigh, "of course not. I have erred in *some* ways. But that's what sacrifice is for."

"Those sins have made you unclean. You need to leave the camp too."

Elihud blinked. Then he expelled a soft breath. "You are a bold one."

"We're all unclean in God's sight, rabbi. As unclean as that beggar sitting by the gate outside—"

"Then why—" Elihud spoke through gritted teeth, "*why* didn't God just cast out the entire camp?"

Matthew blinked. It was a fair question. "I don't know."

"Of course you don't. Your words are insolent and uninformed. And did it occur to you," Elihud jabbed a finger at Matthew's chest, "that the law of Moses was given *precisely* so we might be cleansed?"

"No it wasn't."

"Pardon?"

Matthew swallowed. "Moses's Law—the law given by God—didn't make us pure."

Rabbi Elihud leaned back, face contorting. His next words were a shrill whisper. "How can you *say* such things?"

"All the law of Moses accomplished—" Matthew pointed at the scroll, enunciating his next words, "*all* it accomplished was to show us that we were unclean in the first place!"

"Nonsense! Look at the sacrifices—"

"For whom? The pure? The sinless?"

"Of course not. Those under God's wrath could atone for their sins by offering—"

"Sheep? Goats?" Matthew threw up his hands. "They're dumb animals! I don't know what that accomplishes! Blood for blood! Life for life!"

The rabbi's brow furrowed. "Matthew—"

"Tooth for tooth! Eye for eye!" Matthew was practically screaming. "Yet we pay with *sheep*! Goats and bulls! How do they represent *us*?"

"Well, Yahweh is against human sacrifice—"

"Because it constitutes murder. I know. I—" Matthew choked on his next words. "No. None of this makes any sense."

"It most certainly does."

"Sure—unless you think it truly cleanses us."

"How can we enter God's temple if it does not?" Elihud pointed out the window. "How can the high priest enter God's presence every year if he is not cleansed from his own sins?"

"I don't—I don't know." Matthew shook his head. "But maybe—there's something we haven't seen. Maybe there's a way—"

"A way for what? That beggar out there to join us in here?" The rabbi shook his head. "Impossible."

"And that's the problem." Matthew felt a smile forming on his lips. His body was tingling—almost like triumph flowed through his veins. "What kind of God is so weak that he can't cleanse those who need it most."

Elihud gave an exasperated sigh, rolling his eyes. "We've been through this, Matthew. It is *not* about capability. God is holy and just—"

"How—" Matthew held out his hands, touching his tongue to his upper lip, "*how* can a loving God leave us to die?"

"He didn't. He gave us the law of Moses—"

"If God leaves the leper to die, certainly there is justice—but his redemptive word has failed."

"Only to the unclean."

"We are *all* unclean!"

Elihud did not move. His hands were folded on his lap, and he stared at Matthew. "This is really a problem for you, isn't it."

"And it isn't to you? Don't answer that." Matthew massaged his forehead with a thumb and forefinger, closing his eyes. "Maybe you can just carry on with your God who looks after the perfect and righteous. If they exist."

"Of course they exist. And I don't see where this outburst is coming from—"

"It's been building up. For months." Matthew expelled his breath, shaking his head. "Months and months."

Seconds ticked by. Matthew opened his eyes to find Elihud studying him. Matthew cleared his throat. "You really don't get it, do you."

"I'm afraid I don't."

"Of course not." Matthew gave a small chuckle. "Why would you? You think you're flawless. Why would you even *need* to sacrifice?"

"The law commands it—"

"Of course it does. The law assumes we can't follow it consistently."

Elihud gave a small cough. "I'd appreciate it if you stopped interrupting me. You are only my student, after all."

"And I'd appreciate it if—you know what?" Matthew chuckled again, shaking his head. "No. I'm done."

Elihud's eyes widened. "What?"

"I'm done with this whole Pharisee business. You can keep your cleanliness laws, your 'righteousness'—your God."

"*Excuse* me?"

"Find me a deity who can clean the uncleanable. Choose the unchoosable. I'll follow him."

Elihud inhaled deeply. "He wouldn't be worth following. Such a God would not be just."

"Fine. And I agree. A king does not defile himself, after all. And God is so large—and we are so very insignificant. What love do we even deserve?" Matthew put his hands on his knees, muscles tense. "And that's why I'm leaving."

"Because you're upset at God's justice."

"No—his justice is fine. Like you said, he wouldn't be worth serving without it."

"Then what's the problem?"

"Does—" Matthew struggled, fingers clutching at the air, "Doesn't he have redemption too? Where is *that*?"

"He redeems those who follow the law. In fact, the promised messiah is for those who keep the law and—"

"Not good enough!" Matthew was shouting again. "Why even *promise* us a Messiah in the first place? For those who are already clean and righteous? Only the sick need a doctor, rabbi!"

"I—"

"Only the sick!" Matthew slammed the floor with his fist. "I'm done."

Elihud stared, speechless. He gave a small shake of his head. "So you are."

Matthew got to his feet. He strode to the door—then glanced back. "Any God who can't save me is not one I will serve. Even if he deserves it."

"Then join the sinners outside." Elihud raised his chin. "And do not complain when you are judged on the Great Day of the Lord."

"I won't." Matthew's lips curled. "And I'll see you there."

Then Matthew turned and exited the building, his sandals crunching on the dust-laden steps. He tossed the beggar a coin on his way out the gate.

✝ ✝ ✝

The Present

"I told you, I'll have it by next week."

"Rome needs it now." Matthew held out his palm, standing in the doorway. "I don't invent the deadlines, Barsabbas."

"No. But you enforce them." Barsabbas leaned into Matthew's face, his next words a shrill whisper. "Traitor."

"Someone has to collect taxes." Matthew lowered his voice. "Would you prefer it be the Romans? Come on. Give it to your countryman."

"Countryman—" Barsabbas scowled, averting his eyes. His neck muscles tightened as he shook his head. "You want to know something the Romans did? Just yesterday."

Matthew tried not to roll his eyes. "What."

"They took my niece. Only thirteen, betrothed to the son of a good friend of mine."

Matthew expelled a soft breath. "They made her carry some heavy luggage."

"Of course. Weighing at least seventy pounds. And they could carry it themselves, but they're too lazy. So when she couldn't, you know what they did?"

Matthew leaned on the doorway, eyes on the ceiling. "What."

"Well, she won't talk about it. But she was very bruised when she came home that day...and certain parts of her tunic..." Barsabbas's voice began trembling. His fists tightened, and he stared past Matthew. "I hate them. They can get away with anything. Because who will stop them?"

"Their actions are not my responsibility."

"But you *work* for them!" Barsabbas thrust a finger in Matthew's chest. "You take money—you cheat your *own kinsmen*—and give it to them!"

"No. I take what is owed Caesar, with some extra to compensate for my services—"

"You steal from us and give the money we so desperately need to our enemies!" Barsabbas's voice was a hoarse screech. "You're worse than they'll ever be!"

"I am no worse," Matthew's lips curled, and he leaned in, "than you or your niece."

Barsabbas's jaw dropped. "You—"

"And I'm not going to justify myself to you or—" Matthew cut himself off. "Give me the money, please."

Barsabbas's lower lip trembled. "I'll have it tomorrow." He spat on the ground at Matthew's feet. "Now leave."

Matthew pressed his lips together—then turned and strode into the street. What else could he say?

"Unclean! Unclean!"

Matthew nearly jumped. A leper was backing away from him, hands raised. Rags wrapped over his nose and mouth, hair a mop over his face. The man shook his head, rasping, "Unclean."

Matthew blew out his breath, rubbing his forehead with a thumb and forefinger. Unclean. A part of him wanted to reach out and touch the leper—but no. He was "unclean" enough as a tax collector. And anyway, how could touching help?

He made his way along the streets of Capernaum, shaking his head. *Unclean.* His pulse pounded in his temple as he shoved his way between people.

"I tell you the truth."

A man's voice carried over the market square. Matthew kept walking, jaw set. Another traveling preacher.

"Until Heaven and Earth disappear, not the least blot of a pen—not the faintest stroke!—will by *any means* vanish from the Law given by God to Moses."

Matthew stopped. His fists curled, and he gritted his teeth.

"Not the tiniest iota! The Scriptures cannot be broken."

Matthew turned to the preacher. The man was only meters away, one hand raised as he addressed the crowd. "If you break even the *tiniest* one of these commandments—and if you teach others to do the same—" the man chuckled, shaking his head. "Oh, you'll be called the *tiniest* in the kingdom of heaven."

Just what they needed. More legalism. Matthew squeezed between the crowd, trying to edge closer. He could challenge this preacher. Make him think twice.

"But if you practice—and teach—these commands," the man spread his hands, "you will be great in the kingdom of heaven."

Matthew blew out his breath through tight lips. Like anyone could be perfect. How ridiculous.

"Therefore I tell you," the preacher raised his finger, and the crowd leaned in. A smile pulled at the man's lips, his eyes wandering from face to face. "Unless your righteousness *exceeds* the Pharisees and teachers of the law…there's no way you're getting to the kingdom of heaven."

Gasps in the crowd. More righteous than the Pharisees? Matthew heard murmuring.

That's impossible!

Who could do that?

Well, I guess we're all doomed then.

Matthew blinked. This preacher understood. Yes—yes, they *were* all doomed! And there was nothing they could do about it. Unclean, filthy fools waiting to be judged.

"So don't think—no, don't think—that I've come to abolish the Law. Oh no," the teacher chuckled again, shaking his head. "No way. No, I haven't come to abolish the Law or the Prophets." He put a finger to his own chest. "I'm here to fulfill them."

What did *that* mean? Did this preacher actually get it? Did he see what Matthew saw—that the law was incomplete, able to point out uncleanliness but unable to cure it? And…what about the Messiah it pointed to?

Matthew rubbed his chin with a thumb and forefinger. This was most curious.

"Alright, I'm done for now." The man lowered his hands. "I need to preach in other towns too. That's why I was sent, you know."

Why he was *sent*? This preacher spoke in riddles. Matthew cocked his head. This was worth investigating.

The preacher turned and began making his way through the market square. Four men followed—probably his disciples—and Matthew trailed them, gently pushing his way past shoppers.

They came to an alley—and there Matthew spotted the leper he'd seen earlier. The man was still crying out "unclean!"—but at the sight of the preacher, he fell to his knees. The leper put his face to the ground, his hands outstretched. "Master."

The preacher stopped. His eyes settled on the leper, and he held up a hand. His disciples stopped behind him.

"If you are willing," the leper rasped, face to the dirt, "if you are willing, you can make me clean."

If the preacher was *willing*? Matthew scoffed, rolling his eyes. That's not how the Law worked. You touched anything unclean, *you* became unclean. It didn't work the other way around.

The preacher studied the leper, lips slightly parted. He looked as if he was about to cry. "I am willing," he said quietly. Then he knelt down and touched the leper's head. "Be clean!"

Matthew's world shattered.

The leprosy vanished. The man's skin—it was clean! Completely whole! Not a single rash or blemish.

It was clean.

The man sat up. He raised his arms, eyes darting from hand to hand. "I—I'm clean!"

"Tell no one." The teacher raised an admonitory finger. "Instead, go—show yourself to the priest and offer the sacrifices Moses commanded for your cleansing." His next words were soft. "As a testimony to them."

"I'm clean!" It was like the man hadn't even heard the preacher. He leapt up, screaming in joy. Then he sprinted out of the alley. Matthew heard gasps in the marketplace.

"There goes that," murmured one of the disciples.

"And I was really hoping this town would be different," another one whispered.

The teacher stood and faced them—Matthew ducked behind the wall. "Time to withdraw, I believe." The healer's voice seemed weary. "We'll be back in a week, though."

A week. Matthew made a mental note to be at the front of the crowd when that happened.

† † †

A week later

"Suppose one of you has a friend."

Matthew stood in the back of the room—his back pressed against the wall, squeezed in among strangers like a fish caught in a net. He couldn't even move his arms.

"You go to them at midnight and say, "'friend, lend me three loaves of bread.'" The preacher took on a panicked tone. "'A friend of mine on a trip just came to me—and I have absolutely nothing I can set before him!'"

Some murmurs. How rude would that be! No food to give a friend? And one who'd just arrived in the middle of the night from a long journey!

"Then his friend inside answers."

The preacher's name was Jesus. He'd gained traction in the last several months, from what Matthew had heard. Probably from those miracles—though he was a compelling speaker as well.

"The friend says, 'Bro, don't bother me. It's the middle of night! Ugh!'" Jesus gave an exasperated sigh, eyes on the ceiling. "'The door's locked, my children are sleeping beside me—and it took half an hour just to get them wound down, you have no idea—"

The crowd laughed. Jesus's eyes twinkled as he surveyed them. "'It's too much trouble, man. I can't get you anything.'"

A few nods in the crowd. Murmurs of assent. Most of them wouldn't get up either.

"I tell you." Jesus raised his finger. "Though this guy won't give him a *scrap* for the sake of their friendship, he'll eventually get up and give him the whole pantry because of how much the guy is bugging him."

A few chuckles. A smile tugged at Matthew's lips.

"So I say to you." Jesus's smile faded. "Listen to this. *Ask* and it will be given to you. *Seek* and you will find."

A verse came to Matthew—*you will seek me and you will find me when you seek me with all your heart*. The word of Yahweh from the prophet Jeremiah. Matthew nodded.

"*Knock* and the door will be opened." Jesus made a knocking motion. "For everyone who asks receives—he who seeks finds—" here a grin broke across his face, "—and to him who knocks, the door will be opened."

Matthew's brow furrowed. The context of that passage was redemption—Yahweh's presence for those who seek it. Is that what Jesus meant?

"Think about it. Which of you fathers, if your son asks for a fish," Jesus raised his arm, flopping it like a fish, "will give him a snake instead?" The preacher made a hissing sound. A few chuckles. "Or if he asks for an egg, will give him a scorpion?"

The crowd laughed as Jesus pretended to be stung. "Ow! Really, dad?" Jesus pretended to swat something, then frowned. His eyes burned with a new intensity. "If you then—though you are evil," here he let his finger wander across the crowd, "yes, all of you are evil. But you *still* know how to give good gifts to your kids!"

A few people shifted their footing. That was bold to say.

"If you, then, can give good gifts to your kids—even though you're wicked—how much *more* so will God, who is *perfect*, give his holy spirit to those who ask for it!"

Yahweh's spirit? Given to someone? What, like the deity would dwell with them? Matthew scoffed. Ridiculous. First this preacher told everyone they could never be good enough to enter the Kingdom of Heaven—and now all people have to do is ask, seek, knock? This man made no sense.

"So I tell you." The preacher's eyes wandered across the crowd—Matthew could have heard a pin drop. "Knock." Jesus lowered his voice, raising one fist in a knocking motion. "And the door will be opened to you."

A knock on the ceiling. Jesus looked up.

Pieces of the roof were coming down. Cheap ceramic tiling, pretty standard here. And definitely not coming apart by itself.

Tiling fell by Jesus's feet. He arched an eyebrow. "Someone's taking me literally."

No laughter. Everyone stared at the roof as bits of tiling came loose. A hole broke open, and four faces peered down at them. One of them muttered something to the other, and they made the hole wider. Jesus tried to move back as pieces fell on him, but he bumped against the crowd.

Gasps. The opening was being covered by something! It was a stretcher—bulging like someone was lying in it. It came down slowly—jerking as four ropes lowered it unevenly. It halted at Jesus's waist, swinging a little.

Matthew stood on his tiptoes to see over the stretcher. Lying on it—was that a beggar? Only his eyes were moving...was he—?

"He's paralyzed, Jesus." One of the faces peered down at them from the ceiling. "We figured you could...well..."

Matthew shook his head. Now *that* was chutzpah.

"Friend." Jesus's eyes were on the paralytic. He smiled, inhaling deeply. "Your sins are forgiven."

Matthew's jaw dropped. What? This man could forgive sins? Impossible. Only God had that power. That *authority*.

He heard someone clear their throat. Matthew's eyes darted over—great. Pharisees. Not three feet over, standing with their arms crossed. How they could even move their arms in this crowd was beyond him.

"Why are you thinking these things in your hearts?" Jesus rounded on the Pharisees, neck muscles tight. "Which is easier. Tell me."

The Pharisees did not blink. They just stared at him, shoulders tight.

"Is it easier to say, 'Your sins are forgiven,'" Jesus gestured at the paralytic, "or to say, 'Get up and walk?'"

Now that was a question. Matthew smirked. The *claim* to forgive could certainly be made by anyone. But like the command to walk, it was powerless without actual authority backing it.

"But since you're so curious—here. So that you can tell that the Son of Man has authority on Earth to forgive sins…" Jesus turned to the paralytic. "I tell you—" the preacher indicated the doorway with his thumb, "get up, take your mat and go home."

The man's lips parted—and he raised an arm. The crowd gasped as he sat up. His feet dangled over the stretcher's edge—and he hopped onto the floor. "I—I can walk!"

"Yes you can. You believed I would heal you and followed my command." Jesus grinned at him. "Now go home."

"Whoooo! Praise God!" The man leapt in the air, one hand waving. "I'm telling my family!"

He unhooked his stretcher from the ropes, giving another shout. The crowd parted as he shoved his way through them. He gave one last leap as he crossed the threshold. "Hallelujah!"

Now all eyes were on Jesus. The preacher surveyed them, one corner of his lips raised. "So? Which is harder?"

Matthew shook his head. This couldn't be real.

✝   ✝   ✝

"So in everything, do to others as you would have them do to you." Jesus paused, finger raised as he surveyed the market square. "That and the command to love the Lord your God with all your heart, strength and soul—that sums up the Law and the Prophets."

And they were impossible commands. Matthew reclined at his tax collector's booth, inhaling deeply through his nose. No one was perfect.

"So enter through the narrow gate. For *wide* is the gate," Jesus spread his arms, "and broad is the road that leads to destruction—" he slammed a fist into his palm, "—and *many* enter through it."

Some in the crowd shifted their footing. Matthew spotted uneasy expressions. Why would Jesus be telling this to *them*? As Jews, weren't they already members of the kingdom?

A smile pulled at Matthew's lips. This preacher was great.

"But small is the gate—and narrow the road—that leads to life," Jesus made a meandering motion with one arm, "and only a few find it."

No one found it. Not unless this guy knew about it and led them there. Matthew shook his head, rubbing a coin between his fingers. Like that would ever happen.

Jesus's eyes met his. "You there."

Matthew nearly dropped the coin. Jesus was talking to him?

"Yes, you." Jesus held out his hand—then beckoned. "Follow me."

The coin clattered to the ground. Matthew's lips parted as he stared. Jesus was choosing—him? A tax collector? But he'd tried that old Pharisee business before...

Except—back then he'd been the one trying to be clean enough. This man…this "Jesus" asked only for a knock.

The tax collector licked his lips. Though right now, it felt like Jesus was the one doing the knocking.

"Well?"

"Yes." The words flew out Matthew's mouth. He sprang up, dust rising as his stool fell back. "Yes, I—" his words caught in his throat, "—I want to follow you. Jesus."

Jesus grinned at him. "And you will."

Joy flooded his heart. He had something to do! Something he could *actually* do! Matthew, the unchoosable, had been chosen! A glimmer of something he'd never felt before twisted his stomach. *Purpose.* And…

He looked down at his table. And what about his money?

Matthew cleared his throat, focusing on Jesus. "Want to have lunch?"

✝   ✝   ✝

Now *this* was a banquet. Tax collectors—mostly old friends—some family, a few relatives…they'd all come. Matthew raised a cup of wine, laughing. "I'm a disciple of Jesus!"

The other four disciples were sitting on Jesus's other side. Peter, Andrew, James and John. Former fishermen, from what they'd told him. Crazy.

"This is some good wine!" Jesus laughed, dipping his cup in the wine bowl. "You do know how to celebrate, Matthew!"

Uh-oh. Matthew spotted Pharisees entering. He didn't remember inviting them—but he supposed they could come. A corner of his lips lifted. If tax collectors and other riffraff were allowed, why not the teachers of the law?

"This is ridiculous." A pharisee brushed off the front of his rope, his upper lip curling. His eyes settled on Peter.

"Why do you eat and drink with tax collectors and—" his face contorted, as if it was painful just to say it, "and *sinners*?"

Peter's mouth opened—but he said nothing. He turned to Jesus.

Jesus put down his cup of wine, focusing on the Pharisee. "Why even ask?"

"It's a good question."

"It completely misses the point! Why *wouldn't* I?"

"Well isn't it obvious?" The Pharisee indicated his fellow teachers. "Look at the company I keep. What does that tell you about me?"

"That you don't know how to party."

The Pharisee scoffed. "That I have good taste in people! When you eat with someone," he inhaled deeply, fingers clutching at the air, "don't you see? When you eat with someone, you show you support what they do."

"That's how people think of it, anyway." Jesus plucked a piece of bread from his plate, shoving it into his mouth. Tearing off a chunk, he raised his finger. "But when the doctor visits the sick," he began, mouth full, "does he approve of their sickness?"

"Well, no—"

"Then can I visit these people without approving of their disease?"

Matthew stiffened. Jesus was describing his friends as diseased?

The Pharisee's eyebrows went up, and he exchanged glances with his comrades. "So you *know* they are unclean."

"More than just unclean—sick and badly in need of a doctor." Jesus took a sip of wine. He wiped his beard. "They'll die from their sins if they don't get a medic now."

"And you're their doctor, I suppose?"

"That's right. I've come to seek and save them."

The Pharisee scoffed. "You'll become unclean just like them."

"Only if I behave as they do."

"You already are! Look at you—" the Pharisee pointed as Jesus took another sip of wine, "Here is a glutton and a drunkard! A friend of tax collectors and sinners!"

"Oh, I don't get drunk."

"You drink a bit too much for me."

"And should I cry because you're playing a dirge? Dance for your flute?" Jesus shook his head, smile disappearing. "Should I keep the company you tell me to keep and drink the amount you tell me to drink?"

The Pharisee looked taken aback. "Well, you should keep the law—"

"I *am* keeping the law!" Jesus's fist slammed the table. "Don't you get it? Only the sick need a doctor. The sick!"

Matthew's jaw dropped. Those were Matthew's words—from years ago!

"Do you bring a medic to a perfectly healthy person? Of course not." Jesus stood, his chair scooting back. "I have not come to call the righteous, but sinners, to repentance."

The Pharisee raised his chin, lips pressed together. "So you *do* think they should repent. Then why not keep yourself clean? If they decide to repent, let them come to you."

"No." Jesus shook his head vigorously. "No! Can't you see? *No* one comes that way! What good is a doctor who only treats the righteous? He's useless!" He thrust a trembling finger at the Pharisee, teeth gritted. "*You* have to come to *them*! Then they will come to God."

The Pharisee glared at him, wrinkling his nose. He inhaled deeply, chest rising. "Alright then. Defile yourself." Turning from Jesus, he exited the room. His friends followed, heads held high.

Matthew spat on the ground. "Good riddance, eh?"

"No." Jesus's eyebrows creased—and lines of sadness carved his face. "Matthew, they're sick too. They just don't see it."

Matthew blinked. That was true. "I'm sorry, rabbi."

"Don't worry." Jesus smiled at him—but his eyes were still troubled. The preacher dipped his bread into the wine. "You're forgiven."

Forgiven. But how? And how did Jesus make people clean? How did *any* of that work? "Rabbi?"

Jesus finished chewing his bite. "Mm?"

"One thing I still don't understand."

"Just one?" Jesus grinned. "Ask away."

Matthew cleared his throat. How should he phrase this? He didn't want a debate... "The law always requires sacrifice. The shedding of blood. That is justice."

Jesus gave a sharp nod. "Right."

"So..." Matthew licked his lips. "So how can you cleanse people? Or forgive them? Even if you were the—the Messiah, wouldn't that require blood?"

"That's a good question." Jesus put a hand on Matthew's shoulder, biting his lip. Something in his eyes was troubled. "I have to *be* their righteousness, Matthew."

The Lord our Righteousness—the Prophet Jeremiah's words. Referring to the new David, who would rule Israel forever. Matthew's heartbeat quickened. "How?"

"In time you'll see, Matthew. In time."

"What?" That was no answer at all! "So you'll teach us the answer? No king defies justice. And there are many prophecies still to be fulfilled if you are to fulfill the law."

"I know that. Don't worry." Jesus patted his shoulder, inhaling through his nose. "You'll see just how I fulfill them." He released Matthew's shoulder, focusing on the table. "When I am lifted up," his next words were a whisper, "you will see that I am the promised King of the Jews."

08 · To Whom the Scriptures Testify

John 5

2nd Millennium BC

"You're almost ready to go into the promised land." Moses inhaled deeply, leaning on his staff. The people of Israel stood before him, eyes wide as they listened. "And the nations you drive out listen to those who practice sorcery or divination."

A few nods in the crowd. They got it. Or at least, they claimed to. "But as for you," Moses thrust his finger at them, "the Lord *your God* has not permitted you to do so."

"But Moses," someone in the crowd shouted, "how are we going to follow God without you?"

"Yeah!" A woman joined in. "Joshua is fine, but we need someone to show us the way!"

A reasonable request. Moses nodded, lips pressed together. "The Lord your God will raise up for you a prophet *like me* from among your own brothers. You must listen to him."

Murmurs of assent. The people liked that.

"For this is what you asked of the Lord your God at Horeb. Remember? On the day of the assembly, when you said," Moses lowered his voice to imitate their elders, "'Don't let us hear the voice of the Lord our God or see this great fire anymore, or we'll *die*!'"

More nods. The people knew what he was talking about.

"Yahweh told me, 'What they say is good. Since they can't bear to see the fire, I'll interact with them a different way. I will raise up for them a prophet like you, Moses, from among their brothers."

Now most of the crowd was giving him a blank stare. Hadn't God used *Moses* to talk to them? Was Moses still talking about their wilderness wanderings here?

"'I will put my words in his mouth,' said Yahweh—" Moses spread one hand, "'and he will tell them everything I command.'"

A few "oh's" in the crowd. Moses was talking about a covenant! Yahweh putting his words in someone's mouth. Moses's lips tilted. They *nearly* understood. "Yahweh also told me, 'If anyone doesn't listen to *my* words that the Prophet speaks in *my* name, I myself will call them to account.'"

Oh. Now that struck a chord. A few in the crowd shifted their footing.

Moses smiled, leaning forward. "So listen to the Prophet."

✝   ✝   ✝

2 years old

"Don't look back."

Mary held the sleeping Jesus against her bosom, cloak wrapped around her face. Stars twinkled overhead, the crisp air nipping at her fingers. "Are you sure about this?"

"The angel was clear. We're in danger." Joseph stared at her, enunciating his next words. "We have to leave *now*."

"Because Herod is trying to kill us?" Mary shook her head, tears welling in her eyes. Already things were not going the way she'd imagined. "Because of Jesus?"

"Because of him." Joseph focused on the child. "Herod's going to search for Jesus. We *cannot* be here when that happens."

Mary looked down at her child. His eyes were squeezed shut, lips slightly parted. She ran a finger over his cheek, stroking his jawline.

"Mary."

She looked up at Joseph. He put his hands on her shoulders, eyes wide. "We cannot let him find us."

Mary gave a small nod. Nausea clutched at her stomach, and she swallowed. "I know." She glanced at the donkey they'd laden. All their belongings, stuffed in sacks hanging over the creature's sides. Her next words were a trembling whisper. "Yahweh help us."

† † †

"So they have not returned." Herod sat on his throne, leaning forward. One elbow on his knee, chin resting on his fist. "They have disobeyed me."

"What do you want us to do?"

Herod looked past his commander. "Send soldiers to Bethlehem. Kill every boy of two years or younger."

"Two years or—younger?" The commander tilted his head. "What threat could they pose?"

"Did I stutter?" Herod's eyes bulged. "Two years or younger!"

"I—yes sir."

Herod's lips curled as he enunciated his next words. "That age fits the Magi's timetable for the so-called King of the Jews."

The commander's brow furrowed—but he nodded. "Yes, King Herod."

Herod leaned back in his throne as the commander turned to exit. Resting his elbows on the armrests, he raised his chin. "No child," he began, voice barely a whisper, "is going to steal my throne."

† † †

2nd Millennium BC

A baby boy squalled in the house next door. A woman shrieked, "No!"

A soldier's voice. "Give me your boy!"

"He's my baby!"

"Now!"

Jochebed stepped back from the window, heart pounding at her chest. That was her neighbor. Jochebed would be next.

Her eyes settled on the three-month-old child wrapped in cloths in the corner of the room. He was too old to hide. Even now he was crying, whimpering as his little arms waved up and down.

"My child," she whispered, tears welling in her eyes. Her arms shook as she stepped toward him. "I have to save you."

The boy gave a small whimper as she picked him up. She rocked him in her arms, shushing him. "You'll be fine. I'll hide you. You'll be fine."

The boy blinked once, looking up at her. The fingers on one tiny hand opened, unsteady as they reached for her nose.

"Go with Yahweh," she whispered, looking out the back door. "Maybe he will save us."

A papyrus basket—coated with tar and pitch so it could float—waited on the banks of the Nile. She'd been preparing for the last week.

It was time to part ways.

Jochebed set her boy in the basket, tears flowing down her cheeks. One splashed on the child's arm, and he gave a small whimper. "I'm sorry, my son," she began, her lower lip trembling, "I'm so sorry."

"So you're following through with it."

She glanced back to see her daughter standing by the door. One hand on the doorframe, sadness carving her young features.

"I have to, Miriam." Jochebed put her hands together. "Please watch over him. Make sure he finds a home."

"And if I can't?"

"Please." Jochebed put her hand on the papyrus basket. "You must not fail me."

Miriam stared at the boy, mouth open. "Mom—"

"Please!" Jochebed could hear the soldiers approaching. She pushed the basket into the Nile. "Now!"

Miriam jerked her head toward the door as soldiers pounded on it. "Yes, mom."

Jochebed watched her run along the Nile, following the basket's progress. The boy whimpered as his boat bumped along the reeds—but the tar and pitch held, and the basket twirled lazily down the stream.

Jochebed bit on her knuckle, trying to still the shaking. "Go in peace, my child," she whispered.

✝   ✝   ✝

1st Century AD

A blinding light. Joseph squinted into the darkness, raising his hands to cover his face.

"Don't be afraid."

Don't be afraid? Was this—Joseph fell on his knees, face to the ground. "My Lord!"

"I have a message from God."

Joseph's whole body was shaking. He hadn't seen an angel since the warning… "I'm listening."

"Get up, take the child and his mother and go to the land of Israel—" the angel's voice was like pounding thunder, "—for those who were trying to take the child's life are dead."

"Yes, my Lord." Joseph felt sweat roll down his cheek. His eyes were squeezed shut—

He opened his eyes. He was lying on his back, the ceiling above him. His mat soaked in sweat. Mary was sleeping next to him, her breathing soft.

He swallowed—his mouth was so dry! Then he sat up, taking in a trembling breath. Another dream. It had been years…

"Go to sleep, honey." Mary's mumbling was barely coherent. "You woke me up."

Joseph's breathing was heavy. He stared at the wall, trying to still his beating heart. "Mary."

"What?"

"We need to leave Egypt. Now."

Mary groaned, rolling over. "And go where, honey?"

"Israel."

"What?" Mary's brow furrowed. "Herod will kill Jesus!"

"Not anymore." Joseph licked his lips. He could still see the light in his mind… "Herod's dead."

"Huh? How do you know?"

Joseph looked down at her, swallowing. "The angel said so."

† † †

2nd Millennium BC

"And you're sure about this?"

"As—as sure as I can be." Moses grimaced. Not the most confident reply. "The I Am says so, anyway."

"The I Am?" Jethro's eyebrows went up. "Which God is that?"

"Yahweh." Moses cleared his throat. "And besides, I want to see my own people. Maybe some of them are...still alive."

"I suppose..." Jethro considered, stroking his beard. Then he shrugged. "Why not."

"Thank you." Moses hesitated, fingering his staff. His eyes went to the quilt Jethro had made for them as a wedding gift. "Your daughter will be leaving with me."

"And I'm sure you'll take good care of Zipporah."

"M-hm." Moses still remembered the burning bush. The voice like roaring flames...

Go back to Egypt, for all the men who wanted to kill you are dead.

"Moses? You have my permission, you know."

Moses's eyes darted to Jethro. "I know, father-in-law." He tried to smile. "Thank you."

✝ ✝ ✝

The Present

Covered colonnades stood against the rising sun, its rays casting their carved pillars in shadow. Between four colonnades two trapezoid pools stretched, with a fifth colonnade separating the pools like a dam. Their waters stood still, orange in the morning light.

A tiny ripple appeared in the center of the lower pool—like a finger was touching the water, though none could be seen. Or perhaps a bug was moving along the surface—now the ripples were scattering with its motion.

Bubbles rose to the surface. Small cyclones appeared, then dissipated silently. More ripples.

Then the pool lay still.

Just past the divided pool, a gate opened with a creak. Masses stood waiting at its bars, and they rushed forward. Some pushed each other out of the way, ascending the steps to the colonnades.

But camped by the gate, crippled on their mats, the beggars turned to the pool. A few of them pleaded for help—two even raised their hands—but everyone rushed past. One was shouting, "I can be healed! Just get me in the water!"

But as the masses ascended the steps, one beggar wasn't even moving. His fingers twitched once—then he closed his eyes, laying back on his mat. A tear trickled from one eye.

† † †

8th Century BC

"Tell us more about the servant!"

"Yeah, Mr. Prophet!" The boys ran up to Isaiah, hands out. "Tell us about the Servant of the Lord!"

Isaiah smiled, leaning on his staff. He indicated the beggar sitting past them. "Well, the Servant of the Lord took up our infirmities."

"You mean our sicknesses?"

Isaiah nodded. "*All* our weaknesses."

"What about when we're sad?" The other boy ran a finger down his cheek, like it was a tear. "Will he make us happy?"

"Not in the way you'd expect." Isaiah held out his free hand, as if he was holding something. "He will carry our sorrows on his own person."

The boys stared at him, mouths open. "He'll *carry* our sadness?"

"That's right." Isaiah inhaled deeply, looking past them. His eyes met the beggar's. "He'll heal us and carry our tears."

† † †

The Present

Dust rose with each step. Jesus entered the street, approaching the Bethesda Pool by the Sheep Gate. His disciples followed behind, chatting with one another. Masses pressed against them as they walked—all here for the big feast.

"At least they're not begging us for miracles," John said, nudging James. "The last town we visited, I thought we'd never get to breathe again!"

"We might still not breathe," James agreed, eyebrows rising, "except no one begs him on the Sabbath. Good thing, too, as way more people are here for the celebration."

"You know it! As if Jerusalem isn't busy enough already—"

John nearly bumped into Jesus. The preacher was standing before the gate.

"There." Jesus held up a finger. "Do you see him?"

John blinked. Who was Jesus talking about? He followed the rabbi's gaze and spotted a few men lying by the stairs to the pool. "The beggars?"

"They're always here, aren't they." Jesus swallowed, lips pressed together. "Waiting."

"I—I suppose." John glanced at James—his brother shrugged—then turned back to the teacher. Jesus was making his way to one of the beggars, breaking the crowd's tide as he pushed against people.

John's brow furrowed. Poor beggars were everywhere. And Jesus mostly did his healing after teaching a bit—as a special section afterward, where he might even cast out demons.

"It's odd, isn't it." James's voice was a whisper. "Usually people have to bring their sick to Jesus—not the other way around."

"Sure. But why *shouldn't* he approach them?" Matthew came up behind them, indicating the beggars with his chin. "If I could make people clean, I might consider it."

"Either way, the master knows what he's doing."

They turned to Peter. He was staring at Jesus, scratching his graying beard. "Though I sure don't."

Jesus knelt down to the beggar's level. They exchanged words, though John couldn't hear through the crowd. He pushed his way between people, trying to listen in.

"So you've been here thirty-eight years." Jesus's lower lip was trembling. "Thirty-eight years infirm, and you can barely move?"

"I…" The man's dry lips parted, and he groaned. "That's the idea of it. You can ask around if you…if you don't believe me."

"I believe you." Jesus got on one knee, eyes tearing up. "You know, the Israelites wandered in the desert for thirty-eight whole years—plus bits and pieces of two other years."

That was an interesting comparison. John scratched his cheek. The "forty years" was really a summary, wasn't it?

"They needed a Savior to take them to the promised land—to save them from dying in the desert." Jesus held out a hand. "But Moses wasn't chosen to do it. Instead, God raised up a successor."

The man swallowed—then flinched, trying to speak. His next words were a hoarse croak. "Joshua."

"The name is a form of 'Yeshua,' or Jesus. It means 'The Lord Saves.'"

The beggar stared at him, nonplussed. He turned his head to look up at the sky. "Okay."

Jesus bit his lip, edging closer. "Do you want to get well?"

"Sir," he rasped, "I have no one to help me into the pool when the water is stirred. While I'm trying to get in…" His jaw trembled, and he tried mouthing the next words. A tear slid from one eye. "Someone else…someone goes ahead of me…"

"Well don't just lay there then." Jesus smiled. "Get up and walk!"

Walk? John tilted his head. How could someone in that condition—

The man sat up, his sores closing. His face grew warm and full. Even his arms and legs seemed thicker—no longer just skin and bones! He stood up, eyes wide, looking at his arms. "I—I'm healed."

The man bent down, plucking his mat from the ground. He put it under one arm and straightened, turning to Jesus—but the rabbi was gone. Jesus had slipped into the crowd.

John spotted the preacher heading toward him. Smart. Didn't want the crowd to smother him.

But that Jesus had been up to taking that risk in the first place…John shook his head. "Love defines you, doesn't it."

Jesus wiped a tear from his cheek. "As it should for all who follow me."

✝ ✝ ✝

"I actually like the commotion," Rabbi Ithamar stated, strolling across the Temple court. "Tells me people still care about the feasts."

"I suppose." Nicodemus bit his lip. "They might also just be here for the sake of tradition."

"Now come on! Don't be so cynical. They might—" Ithamar's eyes widened as he looked past Nicodemus. "No!"

Nicodemus followed Ithamar's gaze. What was the Pharisee staring at?

"That beggar's carrying his mat! Come *on*! It's a sabbath, you unclean fool!" Ithamar ran over to the beggar, and Nicodemus followed. "Put down that mat!"

The beggar spotted them—and nearly jumped, dropping the mat. Dust exploded from the mat's impact. "What—I—what do you mean?"

"Why are you carrying that mat? It's a sabbath!" Ithamar shook his finger. "The law forbids it."

"I, eh—um…" The man swallowed, eyes darting between them. "It's not my fault. Someone told me to do it."

"And?"

"Um, the—the man who made me well! He commanded me to pick up my mat. Even though it was a sabbath…"

"Made you well?" Nicodemus stepped in. "You were sick?"

"That's—that's right." The man winced under Ithamar's glare. "I'd been sick for thirty-eight years, sitting by Bethesda…"

"And I'm sure you deserved it." Ithamar put a finger in his chest. "Especially with the way you disregard the law."

Thirty-eight *years* of sickness healed? Nicodemus glanced at Ithamar. The rabbi wasn't even phased.

"Well—" the man's hands were shaking as he plucked the mat, and he dropped it again. "I'm sorry—"

"And who healed you? He's breaking the law too." The Pharisee put his fists on his hips. "Come on—give God glory. Tell the truth."

"I don't know!" The man looked almost relieved as he said it, backing away from them. "I didn't catch his name. I swear by the altar!"

Nicodemus's eyebrows went up. Smart healer.

"Honestly." Ithamar rolled his eyes. "These foreigners come from who knows where with no regard for the Torah. Pathetic."

"So I—I can leave?"

"We'll keep an eye on you." Ithamar indicated the mat. "And for now—leave your mat here."

† † †

Midday at Jerusalem. The Outer Court was bustling with visitors—selling goods, buying sacrifices. A typical day in the Temple of Yahweh.

"Found him."

John turned to Jesus. The rabbi was pointing at an area of the outer court. "He's missing his mat, though."

Why Jesus was looking for the beggar at all was beyond John. The master never bothered to look for *any* of the people he healed. But maybe Jesus wanted to give this one a chance to follow him. After all, he'd slipped away before.

Jesus headed over to the beggar, and his disciples followed. The man's eyes widened when he saw Jesus. "Oh! You're here!"

Jesus grinned. "See—you're well again! My name's Jesus, by the way."

The beggar only stared as the teacher held out his hand. "Jesus?"

"M-hm." Jesus was still smiling—but something was wrong. The man wasn't opting to follow him. He didn't really seem grateful. "You are?"

The beggar swallowed—then turned from Jesus. "I—I can't talk to you."

"Wait!" Jesus put a hand on his shoulder—and the beggar stopped. "At least stop sinning. Otherwise, something worse might happen to you."

John shook his head. This beggar was the most ungrateful louse he'd ever seen. And yet—somehow—Jesus still cared.

"I'm sorry." The beggar turned to Jesus, licking his lips. One hand was shaking—and his eyes were darting all over the court. "I can't—I can't talk to you. Thank you for healing me."

Jesus's shoulders fell. Sadness curved his smile, and he inhaled deeply through his nose. "As you wish."

"I—I'm sorry," the beggar repeated, backing away. He turned and began running to the pharisees.

"What?" James came up beside John. "What's he doing?"

Jesus swallowed, staring after the beggar. "He's selling me out."

"Why that—" Jesus held out his arm, and James bumped into it. "He wouldn't *dare*!"

"I think he would." Jesus's voice was unusually low. "The times are evil, my students. Stay alert."

The Pharisees were talking with the beggar. One of them scanned the crowd—but another strolled to the wall, putting his back to it with crossed arms. Three more teachers of the law joined the beggar.

The beggar glanced back at Jesus, pointing with a trembling finger. The Pharisees looked his way—and Jesus swallowed. "Here they come," he whispered.

The Pharisees strode toward Jesus, robes dragging in the dust. Dirt crunching with each step, fists curled. The one in the lead thrust his finger at Jesus. "You! You've broken Shabbat!"

Jesus's eyebrows went up. "No I haven't."

What was Jesus playing at? John's brow furrowed. The Pharisees knew what he had done...

"Don't deny it. You healed a man."

"And is that really breaking the Sabbath?"

"Of course it is." The Pharisee's lips curled. "Healing is work. Work is forbidden on the Sabbath—and you *know* it."

Jesus clenched his jaw. "God is at work, is he not."

"Certainly. But—he's God!"

"Well," Jesus spread his hands, "my Father is always at work then. To this very day—and I, too, am working."

The teachers gasped. Some exchanged glances—but the one in the lead clenched his teeth. "You call *God* your *father*?"

"He's making himself equal to God," another Pharisee mused, shaking his head. "Equal!"

"Oh, this one's a loon," another one said.

"But he heals, doesn't he?" The fourth one arched an eyebrow, arms crossed. "Oh, we know who you are, Jesus. The carpenter from Nazareth who tricks poor, bumbling fools into following you."

John's muscles tensed. They were referring to him and his fellow disciples.

"Hm." Jesus arched an eyebrow. "I take it you're not impressed by the miracles, then."

"Healing a few sicknesses is unremarkable." The lead Pharisee waved dismissively. "I'm sure you manage it somehow."

"Do I?" Jesus stepped toward them, jaw set. "I tell you the truth."

The Pharisees glanced at each other. No doubt they were unaccustomed to being lectured.

"The Son can do nothing by himself." Jesus put a thumb in his own chest. "Nothing! He can do *only* what he sees his Father doing—because whatever the Father does the Son also does."

"So you're really going to stick with this nonsensical claim." The lead Pharisee shook his head. "Fool."

"For the Father *loves* the Son, and shows him all he does."

The teachers scoffed, some rolling their eyes. "Sure."

"Oh, you're amazed now—but to your amazement he'll show the Son much greater things than these!"

"Like what? Raising the dead?"

Jesus nodded. "Just as the *Father* raises the dead and gives them life—" he took a deep breath, "the *Son* gives life to whoever *he* wants."

"Oh, so you're an independent agent? Some servant of your 'Father' you are."

"No—" Jesus shook his head, swallowing, "—no, the Father has simply given me permission to give life to those I choose. And not only that," Jesus raised a finger to keep them from interrupting, "he's given me the task of judgment. The Father himself judges no one—the Son has that job."

More gasps. Now the Pharisees stepped back, eyebrows flying up. Two of them uncrossed their arms, shaking their heads. The lead just stared, lips slightly parted. "How dare you."

"How dare *I*?" Jesus indicated himself, leaning forward. A vein in his temple bulged. "Really? Shouldn't your response be to *honor* me? After all, you honor the Father."

The lead rolled his eyes. "You are not God."

"And if you *don't* honor me," Jesus stepped forward, neck muscles tightening, "you don't honor the Father either—because he *sent* me!"

The other pharisees were shaking their heads. The lead massaged his forehead, expelling a sigh. "Really? And how, pray tell, should we honor you?"

"I tell you the truth." Jesus raised a finger, inhaling deeply through his nose. "Anyone who hears my word and believes him who sent me—that person has eternal life and will not be condemned."

"So you won't judge the fools who follow you, eh?"

"That's right. They have crossed over from death to life."

The pharisees scoffed again, some chuckling. A few whispered to each other.

"Oh, don't be amazed at this." Jesus shook his head, frowning, "don't be amazed. For a time is coming when *all* who are in their graves will hear his voice," Jesus pointed at the sky, inhaling deeply, "and come out!—yes, out of their graves—those who have done good will rise to live, and those who have done evil will rise to be condemned."

The teachers could agree with that, at least. John could see some nodding their heads. But the lead pharisee was still scowling. "And I suppose you'll raise and judge them by your own power?"

Jesus shook his head. "By myself I do nothing." He dipped his head, spreading his hands. "I judge only as I hear, and my judgment is just—for I seek not to please myself but him who sent me."

Now other Pharisees were gathering—a few even circled around Jesus and the disciples. The lead stepped forward, hands pressed together. By now the court was silent, all eyes on the debate. Dust washed their feet, blown by a gust of wind.

"Well. Isn't this appalling." The Pharisee sneered at him. "You think you're equal to God. You think you have the right to judge. But you boast of gifts you do not give, like a cloud without rain."

John recognized the proverb. He opened his mouth—but Jesus, as if reading his mind, held up a finger. The preacher gave a slight shake of his head.

"You want to challenge us? Fine. Show us your proof." The Pharisee squared himself, arms crossed. "What is your testimony."

Jesus stared at him, raising his chin. Another gust tugged at his hair, and he inhaled deeply.

"Well? What is this grand testimony that will prove all your wild claims?"

As if Jesus's healing miracles weren't enough. John balled his fists. This was ridiculous.

"If I testify about myself," Jesus began, lips barely parting, "my testimony is not valid."

The Pharisee gave a slight nod. "Correct."

"Fortunately, there is *another* who testifies in my favor— and I know that his testimony about me is valid."

"Who? John?"

"Well, I believe you sent to John to ask him a few things—and he's testified to the truth." Jesus swallowed, keeping his chin raised. "Not that I accept human testimony, of course. I mention it that you might be saved—that's all."

"John was—" the Pharisee cut himself off, glancing at the other Pharisees. None of them wanted to publicly condemn the Baptist. "He was not a typical person."

"He was a lamp. One that burned and gave light—and for a time, you chose to enjoy that light."

Hadn't some of the Pharisees been baptized by the Baptist? John arched an eyebrow. Is that what Jesus was referring to?

"That demon-possessed fool who subsisted on locusts and honey." The Pharisee kept his voice low. "The testimony of John the Baptist. Is that it then."

"Oh no. I have testimony *much* weightier than that of John. The very work that the Father has given me to finish," Jesus pointed at the ground, stomping at the dust, "The healing, the teaching, the expelling of demons, all that the Father has given me to do—and which I'm *currently doing*, even on Shabbat—testifies to the truth. The Father has sent me."

"So a few parlor tricks and the testimony of a demon-possessed man." The teacher rolled his eyes. "You should've cast out *John's* demon before he got himself thrown in jail."

Their hardness was incredible. John wanted to tear his hair out—he was sure his face was red. How could *anyone* be this stubborn?

"Not only that, but the Father who sent me has *also* testified concerning me. You—" Jesus raised his finger to keep them from interrupting, "you have never heard his voice nor seen his form, and his Word *clearly* does not dwell in you."

Ouch. Jesus was the whole package—full of grace *and* truth. John tried not to smile.

"We have Yahweh's covenant!" The Pharisee thrust a finger at Jesus, jowls quivering. "We have his promises! We have Torah—and have memorized it since our youth! His Word dwells in us, fool!"

"No." Jesus shook his head, neck muscles tightening. "No, you study the Scriptures. You think the words themselves give you life. What about the one they point to? What about the Messiah? Hm?"

"Well—" The Pharisee gave an exasperated sigh. "Of course the Messiah is important..."

"Of course! And so are the Scriptures! You see, the Scriptures testify—about me!" Jesus put a thumb in his own chest. "They talk about me! They are the fourth witness I call to the stand in my defense."

"Fourth?"

"The Father has testified about me through John the Baptist, my works, my teaching—and the Scriptures, which speak of me from start to finish. Yet you *refuse*—" Jesus was shouting, spit flying from his mouth, "you refuse to come to me to have life!"

"Oh? And where do they speak of you?"

"All over the place—and it's obvious! But you refuse to see it."

The teacher of the law chuckled. "And do your blind followers, who fawn over you day and night, see it?"

"I do not accept praise from men." Jesus made an "X" with his hands. "But I know you."

The Pharisee recrossed his arms, raising his chin. "Do you."

"I do. And I know that you do not have the love of God in your hearts."

Some of the Pharisees gasped. The one in the lead did not even flinch. "Really."

"I have come in my *Father's* name—he's the one I try to please. Yet you do not accept me! You refuse—"

"You make insane claims." The Pharisee spread his hands, stepping closer to Jesus. He leaned his face in. "Why should we even entertain the thought of you? We—"

"Yet—" Jesus raised a finger to keep the Pharisee from interrupting again, "yet if someone else comes in their *own* name—oh, you're just fine! You'll accept him, no problem. How many zealots have you secretly hoped were the truth? And they all perished."

"At least they had an idea of what the Messiah was supposed to be."

"They had *no* idea! They did not perceive the Torah as it should be! And neither do you." Jesus pointed at them, his finger trembling with rage. He inhaled sharply between sentences. "You, who study the Scriptures so often! But you refuse to see what they clearly spell out—the true nature of the Messiah!"

"Why would we refuse to see it?" The Pharisee stepped forward, balling his fists. His face was only inches from Jesus's. "What *possible* motivation would we have to miss the Messiah?"

"Because you want praise from men! It's all about you!" More spit flew from Jesus's mouth. His face twisted with rage, a deep crimson. "You want what's convenient for *you*! Your heart is set on yourself and not on my Father!"

"At least we recognize fools!" The Pharisee was screaming too. "Our lives are witnesses to the integrity of each other! Meanwhile, *you* keep the company of tax collectors and prostitutes!" He spat the words out. "Pitiful fools and sinners, with you as their king!"

"How can you believe if you accept praise from one another—" Jesus took a deep breath, holding up his finger, "yet make *no* effort to obtain the praise that comes from the *only* God—the one whose praise matters?"

"We make *every* effort to obtain his praise!"

"You make every effort to obtain *man's* praise! So that you *look* good!" Jesus stepped back, teeth clenched. He made a barring motion with his arms. "But do not think that I will accuse you before the father. No, I'm not your accuser."

"Really?" The Pharisee arched an eyebrow, arms crossed again. "Because you sound like it."

"No…" Jesus took a deep, trembling breath, shaking his head again. "No, your accuser is Moses, on whom your hopes are set."

More gasps. The lead just shook his head.

"If you believed Moses, you would believe *me*—" Jesus pressed a fist to his own chest. "Because he wrote about me!" He pounded his chest with each word. "He wrote—about—me!"

"Where?"

"Read the Pentateuch!" Jesus threw up his hands—then turned away from them, tears welling in his eyes. "Haven't you read it?"

"We've *memorized* it. You're a madman."

Jesus shook his head, then turned back around so the pharisees could see half his face. "But since you don't believe what Moses wrote…how are you going to believe what *I* say?"

"We believe plenty." The Pharisee raised his chin, squaring his legs apart. "It is you who are in trouble with the law."

Jesus clenched his fists. Then he walked past his disciples, dust rising with each step. He raised a hand, beckoning them—and John followed with the others. Silently they made their way out the gate of the Outer Court, feet crunching in the dirt.

John halted outside the gate. He pressed his lips together, glancing back at the distant pharisees.

They were whispering among themselves.

09 · QUESTIONS IN THE NIGHT

JOHN 3:1-21

2nd Millennium BC

"Why did you bring us out of Egypt?" Nahshon clutched his graying hair, face inches from Moses. Spittle flew from his lips, his face a deep red. "To die in the desert?!"

"We led you here, you ungrateful—" Moses cut himself off, closing his eyes. He tried again. "We led you here to bring you to the Promised Land."

"Out of what? Slavery?" Nahshon swept an arm toward his fellow representatives. They stood behind him, arms crossed. "Slavery is better than this scorched desert! We have no bread—or water!"

Moses arched an eyebrow. "You have the manna."

"Manna! Manna every day." The representative rolled his eyes, planting his fists on his hips. "And you know what? We're tired of those miserable wafers too."

"You're tired of God's provision?" Moses's knuckles were white around his staff. He cleared his throat. "I suppose he's not fixing you up a nice dinner every night."

"No—and we're approaching the Red Sea again. We've been wandering in the wilderness for four decades." His next words were an enraged hiss. "*Decades.*"

"That's entirely your fault." Moses turned from the man, eyes on the Tent of Meeting. "You brought this upon yourselves—you who refuse to believe in Yahweh's love no matter what he does."

"Oh, don't act like *you're* perfect! You're just as—" screams echoed from the tents camped around them. The other representatives began murmuring.

Now what? Moses turned to them. "Yes?"

"Snakes!" The representative pointed at the sand past Moses. Five adders slithered toward them, sand rising in wisps as they wound their way between dry brush. Forked tongues testing the air.

"Look behind you." Moses tilted his staff so it was pointing past the man. "It seems Yahweh has heard your complaints."

"What?" The leader spun as six more serpents approached. The other representatives ran, dust scattering from their footfalls. The lead's eyes widened—and he squared his legs, neck muscles tightening like cords as he shook his head. "No. No—Moses! Make it stop!"

Moses tried not to roll his eyes. "As if I control Yahweh."

"I—I'm sorry, okay?" The man backed into a bush— where a snake leapt out and latched onto his hand. He screamed, trying to shake it off. "I can't! I—Moses!"

Would they never learn? Moses made his way to the Tent of Meeting, a heavy sigh escaping his lips. Screams echoed from the camp all around him—screams and hissing. Moses clutched his staff harder, head bowed.

Yahweh was slow to anger—but he did get angry.

✝   ✝   ✝

Nahshon threw himself at Moses's feet, one hand bleeding as he held out his arms. His whole body was trembling. Sweat traced his jawline, his breath coming in short gasps. "We don't want to die," he whimpered, head to the sand, "and we know we sinned."

Moses looked down on him, his free hand opening and closing into a fist. The man's stench filled his nostrils. "How did you sin?"

"We—we spoke against you." The leader swallowed, neck muscles tightening as he turned his head. "You and—and Yahweh."

Moses clenched his jaw. "M-hm."

"So we're sorry." A tear traced its way through the sweat on his cheeks. His body shook as he sobbed. "We're so sorry. We don't want to die."

Compassion struck like needles in Moses's heart. He swallowed. "And what do you want me to do about it?"

"Pray for us." The man looked up at him, arms trembling as he used them to support himself. "Pray that Yahweh takes the snakes away."

"Very well." Moses heaved a sigh, turning from the leader. What else could he say?

He shook his head, eyes on the clouds as he parted the flaps of the Tent of Meeting—the Tabernacle. These were God's people, after all—the Lord's redeemed. And it's not like Moses was perfect.

"Yahweh have mercy on all of us," he whispered.

✝ ✝ ✝

The adders still slithered between dry brush, hissing as they passed mounds of packed dirt. Israelites molded the mounds, burying their dead. Corpses lay strewn about the campsite, eyes vacant. Weeping carried on the desert wind, tears burning on the hot sand.

Moses made his way to the east of the camp, where Judah was camped. In one hand he held his staff, tapping the ground with each step. In the other hand he clutched a wooden pole. At the pole's top a bronze cobra was wound. Its head pointed out, like it was striking at something. Its flaps were stretched wide, its sculpted tongue extended.

Moses stopped in the middle of Judah's camp. Israelites were on their knees beside him, tears trickling down their cheeks as they stared at their snake bites. Moses dropped his staff, took the pole in both hands, raised it over his head—and plunged it into the sand.

"Let this decree be heard." Moses's voice cracked, and he swallowed. "Tell everyone you know. Quickly."

The Israelites turned to look at Moses. A hot wind blasted sand across their backs, and some flinched.

"Yahweh told me, 'Make a snake and put it up on a pole. Anyone who is bitten can look at it and live.'" Moses's eyes turned to the bronze snake. "So look to Yahweh's provision for your sins, and live."

A woman looked up at the bronze snake. She gasped, then glanced down at her arm. The wound had closed—nothing but specks of dried blood remained.

Other Israelites began looking. One by one, their wounds closed up. Color returned to their faces—and in seconds they were running off to tell their family. The word would spread.

Moses bent down, plucking his staff with a sigh. Yahweh had forgiven—as he always did. "You truly are gracious and compassionate," he whispered, straightening. He hefted the staff in one hand, eyes on the sky. "Slow to anger, and abounding in love."

† † †

The Present

Nicodemus paused at the foot of the stairs, one arm on the wall. He leaned his forehead on it, squeezing his eyes shut. What was he doing? This whole meeting was insanity.

He stepped back from the wall, focusing on the stairs. He was so close…no point in turning back, right? And besides, he needed to know.

Nicodemus stepped lightly up the stairs, lifting his robe so it wouldn't drag. He emerged into the crisp night, blinking in the moonlight. Sitting on the rooftop's far end, a Jew with bushy black hair and shaggy beard sat crosslegged. Half his face cast in pale moonlight—the other half shadowed.

Jesus of Nazareth, here for a midnight meeting.

The mystery preacher grinned, beckoning. "Take a seat."

A seat. Nicodemus's eyes darted to the mat set out before the preacher. He made his way to the mat, ears alert for any noise. If the other members of the Sanhedrin caught wind of this meeting…

"Welcome." Jesus set his hands on his knees, inhaling deeply. "I'm glad you came."

"I'm glad you agreed to this meeting."

"Of course. Seek and you will find."

Nicodemus took a seat, biting his lip. From here, he could see the shadowed half of Jesus's face. The preacher was studying him, though his smile was steady. Nicodemus cleared his throat. "I wasn't even sure you'd agree to this, to be honest."

"Don't be silly." Jesus waved dismissively. "You're a seeker. I will always come to those who search."

"Right. The seekers." Nicodemus swallowed, averting his eyes. It would be easy to pretend he was here on official business…say he was asking questions for the sake of the other Pharisees—but no. He had to be honest. He met Jesus's eyes. "I need to know."

"Know what?"

"Who you are."

A corner of Jesus's lips lifted. "Who do you think I am?"

The man was testing him. Nicodemus laced his fingers on his lap. "Rabbi…" He took a deep breath. "Well, we know you're a teacher who has come from God."

"Do you really?"

"I do. No one else could do the miraculous signs you do if God were not with him."

Jesus arched an eyebrow. "Someone's noticing."

"Indeed." Nicodemus hesitated. "*I* know that you are from God. Many of my fellow Pharisees know it too—but they're afraid to say it."

"I tell you the truth." The preacher raised a finger. "*No one* can see the Kingdom of God unless he is born again."

That was abrupt. Nicodemus hadn't been talking about the kingdom of God—or had he? Maybe this preacher was cutting to the chase. To the heart of Nicodemus's real question. "Born again."

"Yes. Without that, no salvation."

Did this preacher *always* have to speak in riddles? "But how can a man be born when he is old?" Nicodemus held up a palm. "Surely he cannot enter a second time into his mother's womb to be born!"

Jesus shook his head, smile fading. "I tell you the truth." He pointed at Nicodemus. "*No one* can enter the kingdom of God unless he is born of *water* and the *Spirit*."

Nicodemus's lips parted as he understood. "Ah…you mean a purification. Like the rituals in beloved Torah which will cleanse an individual so he can enter the presence of God."

"The place where God rules—his kingship, or kingdom."

"So a different kind of birth."

"Right. Flesh gives birth to flesh, right?" Jesus's eyebrows went up, and he cocked his head. "Likewise, spirit gives birth to spirit. What you are born of defines who you are."

"So if I wish to be saved from God's wrath…"

"If you want your spirit to be saved, you must—" Jesus thrust his finger into Nicodemus's chest, "you *must* be born again."

"Of water and the spirit."

"Water and the Spirit. Yep. So don't be surprised when I say, 'You must be born again.'" Jesus shook his head. "All life requires birth. New life requires new birth. Spiritual life requires spiritual birth."

"And how do we obtain this spiritual birth?"

"Well, look at the wind." Jesus motioned at the sky. He let his hand fall to his lap. "Just as I say that, it stopped blowing. Oh, there it is." A smile tugged at Jesus's lips, the wind tugging at his bangs. "See that? It comes and goes, and blows wherever it pleases. You hear its sound," Jesus cupped a hand to his ear, "Ope! There it is! But you don't know where it came from or where it's going."

"Indeed."

"So it is with everyone born of the Spirit." Jesus held his hands out. "The Spirit, like the wind, is not so easy to predict or understand—and neither are those born again."

"You speak in so many riddles."

Jesus shrugged. "My sheep will hear my voice."

"Some would call that an excuse for being overly enigmatic."

"Others might call it separating the wheat from the chaff—the people who aren't born of the Spirit won't get what I'm saying." Jesus scratched his chin. "And I'm fine with that."

"So your words are only understood by those who believe them."

"Yes. Quite a paradox, isn't it?"

Nicodemus gave a small sigh. "And supposedly we can't even *see* the kingdom of God—"

"—that is, his kingship—"

"Right, his kingship—unless we are born again through a sanctifying process that regenerates our spirit."

"Exactly!" Jesus held out his arms as if offering a hug. "Which operates like the wind. Mysterious and unrestrained by human will."

Nicodemus was trying not to scoff. "How can this be?"

"How can it *not* be?" Jesus shook his head. "You're Israel's teacher, for crying out loud—but you don't get this! It's shown all over the Scriptures!"

"And where is it directly stated?"

"Ezekiel's prophecy. Right before the Valley of Dry Bones incident. Do you remember something about sprinkling water to cleanse Israel—something about God's spirit?"

Wait…Nicodemus pulled on his ear. "I do, in fact."

"Excellent. Can you tell me about it?" Jesus leaned forward, gesturing with an open palm. "I want it in your voice."

His voice. Nicodemus cleared his throat. "Very well. Yahweh was speaking through Ezekiel, telling Israel that he will redeem them for his sake."

"And it's clearly a redemption from their sins—not simply their earthly enemies."

"Correct." Why emphasize that? Nicodemus cleared his throat again. "Ezekiel, speaking by the spirit of Yahweh, went on to say this…"

6th Century B.C.

"Then the nations will know—will *know*—" the prophet Ezekiel slammed his fist into his palm, "that I am the Lord, declares the Sovereign Lord, when I show myself holy through you—" he pointed at the exiled Israelites before him, dirty beggars in rags, "before their eyes."

The Israelites were just staring. Mouths open, eyes wide. They always found his words interesting—but they never really listened.

"For I will take you out of the nations—I will gather you," Ezekiel made a gathering motion with his hands, "from all the countries and bring you back to your own land." He pointed in the distance, as if they could see Israel from here. "You'll be redeemed."

Still nobody spoke. Water trickled gently beside them, and one dipped his hand into the stream.

Ezekiel scratched his shaggy beard, inhaling deeply. The water would be a good illustration. He stepped over to the stream—and dipped his dirt-caked fingers in. Raising them above one boy, he flicked the water off. "I will sprinkle clean water on you, and you will be clean."

The boy jumped back, gasping. He blinked at Ezekiel, swallowing. "Clean from what?"

"I will cleanse you from all your impurities and from all your idols." Did they get it yet? The real thing God was saving them from? "I will give you a new heart," Ezekiel pounded his chest with both fists, "and put a new spirit in you."

"What's wrong with the one we have?" a woman shouted from the audience.

"Is Yahweh going to recreate us?" A man put his fists on his hips. "We already have a spirit."

Ezekiel elected to ignore them. "I will remove from you your heart of stone and give you a heart of flesh."

"So—we'll be completely new people?"

"The man wants us to be born again!"

"No, better than that—he says *God* will *remake* us!"

Ezekiel clenched his teeth—then let his muscles relax, closing his eyes. Best not to respond. "I will put my spirit within you," he continued, eyes fluttering open as he bent down. He blew on the sand, and granules took to the air.

"And move you to follow my decrees and be careful to keep my laws."

"And we'll be back in Jerusalem?"

He nodded at one woman. "You will live in the land I gave your forefathers." He raised his finger to keep them silent. "You will be my people, and I will be your God."

A statement of covenant. They stared at him as he straightened. Ezekiel put one hand on the boy, jaw set. "I *will* save you from all your uncleanness."

The Present

"Exactly." Jesus grinned. "God will put a new spirit in you—you will be born again of the spirit."

"But how will Yahweh accomplish this?"

"Oh come on!" Jesus threw up his hands. "I tell you the truth." He put his hands on his knees, leaning forward. "You say '*we* know you are a man of God.' As if the other pharisees know! Well, *this* 'we,'" he plunged a finger into his own chest, "speaks of what *we* know, and we testify to what we have seen—but still you people do not accept our testimony!"

"I'm willing to consider it." Nicodemus raised his chin. "And I'm here, aren't I?"

"Yes—but..." Jesus licked his lips, holding out his hands as if they could explain. "Look. I've been speaking to you about these earthly things—being born again, how God's spirit cleanses mankind so they can enter God's presence—but you won't believe me. So how are you going to believe me when I speak of *heavenly* things?"

"Believe?" Nicodemus's eyebrows shot up. His chest rose as he took a deep breath. "Well, I don't know. I am more than willing to consider your assessment of what it *takes* to get to heaven, but—"

"No one has ever ascended into Heaven," Jesus declared, leaning forward, "*no one*—except the one who came from Heaven. The Son of Man."

The Son of Man. That figure in Daniel's prophecy… "The Messiah."

"That's right. No one else has done it."

"But we have kept the Torah since we were children," Nicodemus objected, rubbing his beard, "so wouldn't we pass into Heaven? Why should we need to be 'born again' into spiritual life—through water, spirit or any other means? Many of us would say we are already there."

"That's where you're wrong. As we see in the scroll of Ecclesiastes, 'There is not a righteous man on earth who always does what is right and never sins.' And—" Jesus raised his finger to keep Nicodemus from interrupting, "and as David writes, 'There is no one who does good.' The Prophet Isaiah even adds, 'We all, like sheep, have gone astray—we have, every one, turned his own way.'"

"Fair enough. But that's why the law exists." Nicodemus laced his fingers again. "As a provision for our sin."

"The law does lay the *foundation* for a provision," Jesus conceded. "But the law itself does not solve the problem."

"Sacrifice is not sufficient?"

"Oh, it's sufficient. Depending on what you sacrifice."

"Naturally," Nicodemus waved dismissively, "and I wouldn't suggest that a blemished sacrifice could ever clear sin—"

"But they're all blemished. Aren't they." Jesus was frowning now. His eyes burned into Nicodemus, his neck muscles tight. "Every single Passover lamb. Right since the beginning, they've all been imperfect."

"Well—" Nicodemus threw up his hands, giving an exasperated sigh, "certainly. Otherwise we wouldn't have to keep offering them every year, now would we?"

Jesus's eyes twinkled. Apparently Nicodemus had said just the right thing. "You got it," the preacher said, shaking his fists excitedly, "we need a completely perfect sacrifice! But only one entity in all existence is perfect."

"Yahweh."

"That's right. So what sacrifice is needed?"

Nicodemus's brow furrowed. "You're not suggesting the Messiah—the Son of Man—will sacrifice *himself?*"

"Why not? Just as Moses lifted up the bronze snake in the desert—" Jesus raised one hand, eyes on the hand, "so the Son of Man must be lifted up," he raised his other hand, so that his arms were spread like he was on a cross, "in order that everyone who believes in him may have eternal life."

"Truly?" Nicodemus shook his head. He ran a thumb along his fingers, inhaling deeply through his nose. "And you are that Son of Man."

"What do *you* think?"

"I think…" Nicodemus hesitated, scratching his chin. His eyes fell to Jesus's feet. "I think there are still some prophecies for you to fulfill."

Jesus nodded. "Granted."

"But—I will be watching." Nicodemus got to his feet with a grunt, the sand on their rooftop scraping under his sandals. He expelled a soft breath. "Especially for that perfect sacrifice part—when you are 'lifted up' as a provision for sin."

Jesus did not smile. The lines of his face seemed deeper—almost haggard. "I know you will."

> *For God so loved the world that he gave his one and only son, that whoever believes in him shall not perish—but have eternal life.*

2nd Millennium BC

"Are you done yet, Moshe?"

"Give me a second, Lydia!" Moshe stood on a stool by the doorway, holding a piece of brush dripping with blood.

He scraped it over the top of the doorframe. "I'm almost ready."

"Alright. Hurry!"

Moshe passed the brush over the left frame. Scratches of blood fled the brush's twigs, crimson streaks gleaming in the setting sun's light. Would that be good enough for the Lord? "One more stroke."

He passed the brush over the right side of the doorframe—there. Then he turned to the setting sun. Already the land of Egypt was bathed in darkness just outside Goshen—courtesy of the ninth plague. In minutes dusk would settle on this house.

Moshe hopped down from his stool and ran inside. The Lord would see that blood, right?

For God did not send his son into the
world to condemn the world—but to save
the world through him.

Bitter herbs. Bread without yeast—these were the commanded ingredients to go with their Passover Lamb. The father shoved meat into his mouth, cloak tucked into his belt. His other hand clutched a staff.

Moshe had his own staff too—and now his knuckles were white as he gripped it. He stuffed a piece of lamb into his mouth, fingers unsteady. Moses had been clear about Yahweh's command.

Eat it in haste.

His eyes darted out the doorway, where shadows lengthened along the street. The blood was enough, right?

Whoever believes in him is not
condemned—but whoever does not
believe stands condemned already,
because he has not believed in the name
of God's one and only son.

Locusts chirped in the night. Houses lined the dirt road, some with scratches of blood on their door posts. The windows were dark, their light long extinguished.

Darkness pooled on the street, like a shadow being cast. Or perhaps not a shadow—it was more as if whatever cast it was so bright that, even though its light could not be seen, everything around it seemed darker. The darkness crept along, coming to the first house.

Scratches of blood lined the door posts. The unseen light moved on.

The next house did not have blood. The doorpost blackened as the unseen light entered through it.

> *This is the verdict: light has come into the world—but men loved darkness instead of light, because their deeds were evil.*

The pharaoh sat on his throne. Leaning forward, elbow on one knee, chin on his fist. Staring into the darkness.

Only feet away a torch burned, unseen sparks flying from it. Yet the void of the ninth plague closed around the pharaoh, clutching at his body like strands of rope. Still he stared into nothing, jaw clenched.

Hard lines carved his face. Rigid furrows traced his lips, running up to his raised nose. Weary lines ran along his forehead.

His lips curled ever so slightly. The darkness would not yield. But neither would he.

> *Everyone who does evil hates the light, and will not come into the light for fear that his deeds will be exposed.*

The unseen light approached a new house. Its light was still burning—and just inside the door, three people sat in a circle. Holding hands, whispering as they prayed.

The darkness stopped before the doorframe. Blood was scratched on its sides and top, a darkened crimson against the wood. The unseen light moved on.

Inside the three people kept praying, eyes shut, squeezing each other's hands.

> *But whoever lives by the truth comes into*
> *the light—so that it may be seen plainly*
> *that what he has done has been done*
> *through God.*

FOR DEEPER STUDY

BIBLE STUDY GUIDE

for Individuals and Small Groups

Want to go deeper? These questions are meant to spur thought and spiritual development, and are intended to be used as you study the Word of God alongside these dramatizations. The questions can be used individually or in a small group setting.

I pray God opens your eyes to his glorious identity and gives you wisdom as you prayerfully undertake this study.

A VOICE IN THE DESERT • DEEPER STUDY

John is an interesting figure in history. He grew up in the Qumran community, an ultraconservative sect of Judaism which believed in asceticism (refraining from earthly pleasures), extreme modesty and memorization of the Scriptures—word for word, every inch of every scroll—from youth. They lived out in the desert, and their belief was that the Jewish race's goal was to keep itself from being polluted by outsiders until the Messiah came. As a result, isolation was their primary way of life.

Furthermore, it is likely John would have known Jesus since childhood. (Though he would not be aware of Jesus's status as Messiah until now.) Qumran was close to where Jesus grew up, and there was prohibition against mingling with fellow Jews.

It is interesting, then, that John comes at a time when God has been silent for 400 years (since Malachi). Out of the desert—out of silence, out of wilderness—God begins speaking to Israel again. And John is his instrument.

John Preaches Repentance

John 1:1-34; Luke 3:1-18

1. We all have a purpose in life. What was John's purpose?

   How did John's upbringing and circumstances make him fit for this purpose?

2. What is your purpose in life?

3. How does John bring purpose to his audience?

4. Read Isaiah 43:21. Why does purpose matter to God?

5. If you were standing on the shores of the Jordan asking, "What about me? What should I do?" What do you think John would say to you?

Malachi Chastises the People

Overview of Malachi, particularly 1:1-14; 2:1-9, 17; 3:1

6. Is Malachi's behavior toward authority acceptable here? Why or why not?

   When is it appropriate to exhibit this behavior in your own life?

7. What is God's purpose for people like Malachi—and how does it compare to John's purpose?

8. As the writer, I don't simply insert flashbacks randomly. They're always related to the event I'm dramatizing. So what is the relationship between the Malachi flashback and the dramatization?

The Baptism of Jesus

Matthew 3:1-17; Mark 1:1-11; Luke 3:21-23; Isaiah 42:1

9. What does it mean to "prepare the way"?

10. Why bother with a messenger to "prepare the way"? Why couldn't Jesus simply prepare his own way?

11. For what reasons would Jesus want to be baptized?

12. What would your reaction be if Jesus asked you to baptize him?

THE TEMPTATION OF JESUS •

DEEPER STUDY

Jesus was clearly going through Deuteronomy in his devotions at the time the devil tempted him. All his responses come from that book. He could have simply told Satan off, saying, "You're wrong! Scram!" right from the get-go. But he didn't. Scripture instead shows us a savior who relied upon Scripture.

But why? After all, Jesus is "the Word made flesh." So what's the point?

Remember that Jesus is setting an example for us to follow. He is telling us that the Word of God is always the ultimate authority—the ultimate defense against the devil's temptations.

Temptation #1: Stone to Bread

Matthew 4:1-3; Mark 1:12-13; Luke 4:1-3

1. Read 2nd Chronicles 16:7-9. What's the real sin here if Jesus turns the stone to bread?

2. When have you been tempted this way in your own life?

...But on Every Word

Deuteronomy 8:1-5

3. "Man does not live on bread alone, but on every word that comes from the mouth of God." How do you apply this mentality to your own life?

Temptation #2: Leap of Faith

Matthew 4:4-6; Luke 4:4, 9-10

4. Read Jeremiah 23:29; Hebrews 4:12. Satan can "use" Scripture too! How can God's words have power to fight Satan, then? How can the Word have power at all?

5. Read John 14:26; 1st Corinthians 2:12. When have you been tempted to distort the Word of God to suit your own views? How can we avoid doing this as believers?

Testing at Meribah

Deuteronomy 6:16; Exodus 17:1-7

6. Read Psalm 78, focusing on vv11-24. What is the deeper sin of the devil's second temptation?

7. Read Psalm 77:10-12. What strategy can you use to trust God more?

8. As the writer, I don't simply insert flashbacks randomly. They're always related to the event I'm dramatizing. So what is the relationship between the water from a rock flashback and the dramatization?

Temptation #3: All the Kingdoms

Matthew 4:7-11; Luke 4:12, 5-8, 13

9. This temptation is more "obvious" than the others in that it is clear that what the devil asks is a sin. Nonetheless, Christians are just as guilty of succumbing to it as they are to the other two. What is the deeper sin here?

10. Read 1st Thessalonians 5:16; Revelation 14:9-12; Romans 12:1. What are some ways we can guard against rationalizing our way into this sin?

11. Read Jeremiah 31:32-34; Isaiah 42:6-7 (quoted in this dramatization). 40 years in the wilderness for the

Israelites. 40 days in the wilderness for Jesus. What is the significance of Jesus's experience being a parallel to that of the Israelites?

12. Why was it necessary for Jesus to experience temptation in the first place?

Too Small a Thing • Deeper Study

God loves to teach by speaking in riddles. Jesus often doesn't like to say things in an obvious manner; he wants you to think about it to understand what he's saying. So we see him say, "the water I give him will become in him a spring of water welling up to eternal life," and he refers to "living water." By forcing us to figure out what he's saying, Jesus is actually teaching *more* effectively—as our minds are required to create solutions in order to understand the teaching, fostering engagement and internalization rather than mindless memorization and regurgitation. This is an extremely effective teaching method, and Jesus uses it throughout his ministry.

But there's so much more than just his teaching style to study here. This is top-grade evangelism at work. Here Jesus he shows that he can transcend even the most rigid cultural barriers—men speaking to women, Jews speaking to Samaritans. No barrier will stop the Word made Flesh.

Jonah's Anger at God

Jonah 4; also refers to 2:9

1. What is the deeper reason Jonah is angry at God?

2. How does "salvation belongs to the Lord" serve as a theme for the book of Jonah?

3. When have you had difficulty extending God's grace to others? What can help you?

Jesus at the Well with Sariah

John 4:4-26

4. Read John 7:37-39. What is this "living water" Jesus speaks of?

5. Why is it important that Sariah brought up Jacob— the one whom God renamed "Israel" and instated the Old Covenant with?

6. Though Sariah is a sinner (like all of us), Jesus does not refuse to speak with her. However, why ask her to get her husband when he knows that this will lead to pointing out her sin?

7. Read John 3:20. Some people will immediately close up when you mention their sin, as they'll assume

you're judging them (or get defensive because they judge themselves). But Sariah opened up *more* after Jesus mentioned actions that, in their society, would have been considered shameful. What insight can we gain into the psychology of spiritual seekers?

8. Where do we worship God? Jesus seems more concerned about *how* we worship God. By that metric he identifies the true church—not a building, but a *people* worshipping God "in spirit and in truth." But what does it mean to worship God in spirit and in truth?

Jonah Talks with Amos

Amos 3:2, 8; 4:4-11, 13; 5:14; 7:4-6, 10-15; 9:9-12

13. In Amos's day, the ancient world was filled to the brim with "yes-men" prophets. Ancient sources tell us that prophets usually told their kings exactly what the royalty wanted to hear. Moreover, prophets gained their living from the charity of society—much like a street musician—and often received more contributions for good prophecies. Read Jeremiah 5:30-31; 23:25-29; 2nd Timothy 4:3-4. Where do we see these "prophets" today?

14. "The land cannot bear all his words." (Amos 7:10) Compare to Jeremiah 6:10. Where do we see this in our own society?

15. How does our relationship with God make us *more* accountable to him?

16. In what context can God's judgment be an act of mercy?

17. Read Acts 15:12-18, which quotes Amos 9:11, 12. What does it mean to you that God's plan from "ages past" was to make the Gentiles part of his people?

Sariah Tells the Town about Jesus

John 4:39-42

18. There's an irony here. The promiscuous woman of the town, who has to draw water at midday to avoid the reproach of her neighbors, is now the evangelistic tool Jesus uses to draw people to himself. What can we learn from this?

Too Small a Thing (Servant Song)

Isaiah 49:5-6

19. Why is it "too small a thing" to save only Israel?

20. What does this show about God's character?

A Prophet Without Honor •
Deeper Study

Ever wondered what it was like for Jesus to visit home? His neighbors knew him back when he was a toddler soiling his pants. His own brothers didn't believe in him. His father was dead, and as far as the town knew Joseph and Mary had conceived Jesus while they were still engaged.

And here he is, after a fruitful ministry of preaching literally everywhere else. Only to come home and be sneered at by his own neighbors. As far as they were concerned, he should have stayed a carpenter.

I think Jesus had a very heavy heart.

Flashback: Jesus at the Temple

Luke 2:41-52

→*Referenced verses include Isaiah 61:1-3a; Psalm 142:7; Jeremiah 5:25; Micah 5:2; Isaiah 2:1-5; Micah 4:1-5; Isaiah 65:25; Isaiah 49:6 (alluded to by Jesus).*

1. What are the differences between the year of the Lord's favor and the day of vengeance?

2. Read 2nd Peter 3:9-10. Why did God separate the year of the Lord's favor and the day of vengeance?

3. We know that Jesus was sinless. But here his parents are clearly grieved because of his actions. How is his behavior okay?

Reunion with the Family

Some kind of reunion occurred (obviously Jesus wouldn't ignore his own family), but it is not detailed in Scripture. Therefore, all the details in this section of the dramatization are interpolated from various sources, ranging from archeology (the stove, ancient carpentry, etc.) to the books of James and Jude (for their respective personalities) and Mark 6:3 (for the names of Jesus's brothers, the apparent early death of Joseph—and Jesus's previous occupation as carpenter). Jesus's conversation with Mary is greatly influenced by Luke 1:46-56; 2:19, 33-35; 22:41-44, along with a general study of their personalities as the Gospels portray them.

4. Read 1st Corinthians 15:7. What finally convinced the brothers of Jesus's real identity?

    If you were in their shoes, what would have been needed to convince you?

5. The word used for "kingdom" is really used to mean "kingship." What does it mean when Jesus says "the kingship of God" is near?

6. Read James 2:1-7; Luke 1:50-53. Why is it so important to Jesus's family that favoritism be excluded?

7. Mary asks Jesus, "Can't you just march in and liberate us now?" Well, why shouldn't Jesus do just that? Why go through all this trouble?

8. Dread, anxiety, angst. All emotions we might see as negative. But the Son of God is recorded as exhibiting such emotions—particularly in the Garden of Gethsemane. Yet these feelings must have been weighing on him all throughout his ministry, building up in severity. Some Christians believe such emotions are wrong. Why is it okay for Jesus—and us—to feel these things?

9. How was it helpful to Jesus to be a carpenter before he began his ministry?

Rejection at Nazareth

Luke 4:14-30

10. How does Jesus fulfill the different parts of the Isaiah passage (61:1, 2)?

11. Why is no prophet accepted in his hometown?

12. How might we let our own pride get in the way of hearing God's truth?

13. Elisha was meant to be a symbol of the messiah just as Elijah was meant to be a symbol of the Messiah's forerunner. Why was the crowd so upset at what Jesus said?

14. What motivates Jesus's compassion, fury, gentleness and indignation?

FOR THE SAKE OF THE CALL •

DEEPER STUDY

When Yahweh calls, none can refuse. With the exception of Luke, the Gospels generally emphasize Jesus's authority when relating his call—he called them, therefore they joined him. Jesus knew just what would get them out of their boat and onto his. He wanted fishers of men—and he knew exactly where to find them.

The call of the disciples is an odd thing, when you think about it. Why these guys? Jesus could have called anyone else. Just what about these fishermen drew Jesus's interest? Their hearts weren't necessarily great—after all, they would all scatter upon Jesus's arrest, and one of them would deny Jesus three times after committing violence in his name. So why were these ordinary fishermen chosen?

Maybe that's the point: they were "ordinary." Ordinary people turn the world upside-down for God—because God has called them to be extraordinary for him.

Elisha is Called by Elijah

1ˢᵗ Kings 19:19-21

1. How would you have reacted in Elisha's shoes?

2. In what ways has God called you?

3. Why burn the plowing equipment and kill the oxen? Elisha could have just left without doing anything to his equipment. What's the point?

4. Rushing to join Elijah without a solid financial plan might have seemed like foolishness to everyone else—especially considering the danger Elisha was putting himself in. What factors justify Elisha's decision here?

You Have to Count the Cost!

Luke 9:57-62; 14:25-35

5. What does it mean to "count the cost"?

6. Jesus uses two illustrations. Both of them seem to indicate that if you can't afford it, don't do it. This doesn't seem very seeker friendly—so what is the point of Jesus using these illustrations?

7. What is the significance of Jesus's call being more immediate than Elijah's call?

8. Why does Jesus use such extreme language?

9. What is the purpose and significance of Jesus renaming Simon "Peter"? (I don't just mean the meaning of "Peter." I mean the significance of renaming someone to begin with.)

Call of the disciples

Luke 5:1-11

10. What is the point of telling the disciples to cast their nets on the other side if Jesus's plan is to abandon the catch anyway? What does this show about God's character?

11. No declaration of Peter's sin has been made. Yet he throws himself at Jesus's feet and calls himself unworthy. Why?

    What does this show about Peter's heart?

12. What a waste of fish! And PETA would surely be outraged at the cruelty of letting them die in such a way. How would you justify this?

13. What does God require of us as believers?

THE MISSION OF JESUS • DEEPER STUDY

Purpose. It defines us—and God created us for it.

When Jesus came to earth, he had a purpose. Every action was deliberate—every word intentional. He displayed a singular focus that most of us will never even begin to understand. But he also slept, retreated to lonely places and drank wine at parties (for which some called him a drunkard). These too served his purposes.

What must it have been like to be in that synagogue? To hear the passionate preaching of the divine. And then witnessing an unprecedented victory over evil when the demon possessed man came in. I would love to have been there.

But here we are in the 21st century—and we'll just have to imagine the details.

Praying in the Morning

Luke 5:16 (see also 4:42)

1. Why did Jesus retreat to quiet and lonely places? After all, he is always in communion with the father. Of all people, he would need quiet time the least.

2. What significance does Jesus's example have for us?

Isaiah before Ahaz

Isaiah 9:1-7

3. "But in the future [God] will honor Galilee of the Gentiles." How did God do this?

4. In the ancient world, a light dawning was indication of a deity's presence. Why is it significant that the light dawns on those living "in the land of the shadow of death"?

5. What does Ahaz's attitude toward Isaiah's prophecy—especially in regard to military victories—indicate about human psychology?

6. Why does it matter that our own hearts be changed by God? Why *not* just conquer and bring in an earthly dominion?

7. "Wonderful counselor." Literally this means "wonder counselor," as in, "counselor whose name is wonder" or "wonder of a counselor." "Wonder" in the biblical since is not used to mean mysticism or puzzlement, but far-reaching wisdom that is beyond our understanding. (See also Job 42:2-3.) Read John 14:16-17; 26. What does this mean for us as believers?

8. What does it mean that God is heroic?

9. Read Romans 8:15. What does it mean that God is our father?

10. Peace is not the absence of fear, but the presence of God. Read Judges 6:24. What does it mean that God is the Prince of Peace?

Casting out the Demon in the Synagogue

Luke 4:31-37; references Isaiah 66:2b

11. The beatitudes flip the world's values upside-down while showcasing God's values. What does the kingship of God value—and what does this show about God's character?

12. If the poor are so valuable to God, why are their lives so miserable?

13. Why is it specifically the downtrodden of society that are highlighted here?

14. Why does Jesus order the demon to be quiet?

15. Why is it important that Jesus taught with authority?

16. Should we emulate his example here? Why or why not?

THE SAVIOR OF THE UNCLEAN •
DEEPER STUDY

God is holy. This means, among other things, that the unclean is burned up in his presence. And while this satisfies God's justice, his redemptive power is called into question if those he desires to save cannot even approach him.

Back when the Prophet Isaiah was called, he saw God and said, "Woe to me! I am ruined! For I am a man of unclean lips, and I live among a people of unclean lips, and my eyes have seen the King, the Lord Almighty." But a seraph took a live coal from the altar and pressed it to Isaiah's lips. The angel said, "See, this has touched your lips; your guilt is taken away and your sin atoned for."

Something was different. Instead of Isaiah being burned up in God's presence, God had purified and claims Isaiah.

This would not be the last time such a pattern was set forth in the prophet. And when it comes to atoning for sin, it was nowhere close to the first time either. Throughout the Bible, sinners are allowed to enter God's presence if they are first cleansed.

Yet how can we cleanse ourselves? We are in desperate need of a savior who cleanses us by touching us with the product of the altar where he was slain. We need the Savior of the Unclean.

Note: Due to the length of this dramatization, you may find it better to split this session into two studies.

I pronounce you clean

Leviticus 13:38-39, 45; 14:1-7

1. What was the point of the command to cry out, "Unclean!" Whom did it benefit?

   What does this command show you about God's character?

2. The cleansing ritual involves dipping a live bird into the blood shed by another bird. As believers in the New Testament era, we have a better understanding of the significance of this act. What is it symbolic of—and how does that relate to cleansing?

3. Scarlet yarn, hyssop and a piece of wood are also involved. What is the symbolic value of these elements in the ritual?

4. The live is bird is then released. Why?

5. Using this ritual, how would you explain the Gospel to an unbeliever?

Matthew's debate

(The passage being read in the opener is Numbers 5:1-3)

No one really knows Matthew's past. However, his familiarity with the Scriptures indicate some kind of past with it, and the fact that he is a tax collector at the time Jesus calls him means he was in a bad position with the Israelites. To willingly choose that profession with so much knowledge of Scripture indicates total disenfranchisement. Add to this that he was ready to follow Jesus and you have someone who was searching but had given up thinking he would ever find anything. I think this debate (or something like it) is plausible.

6. What is Matthew primarily upset about in this debate?

7. What does the commands about cleanliness show us about God's character?

8. What about the rituals to *become* clean?

9. The rabbi debating Matthew really makes only three scripturally unsupported assertions here—one regarding the Messiah, one regarding those with permanent skin diseases, and one regarding his own state before God. What Scriptures would you use

(from the Old Testament) to combat his misperceptions?

10. Matthew makes the objection, "Tooth for tooth! Eye for eye! Yet we pay with *sheep*! Goats and bulls! How do they represent *us*?" What is the substance of the objection being made?

How does the Gospel satisfy this objection?

If you are willing

Luke 5:12-15; Matthew 8:1-4; Mark 1:40-45

11. Matthew was seen like a defector. The equivalent today might be a Nazi sympathizer among the Jews fleeing the wrath of Hitler. How would you have viewed such a person?

12. "Until Heaven and Earth disappear, not the least blot of a pen—not the faintest stroke!—will by *any means* vanish from the Law given by God to Moses." What does this mean?

13. "The Scriptures cannot be broken." As the Word Made Flesh, Jesus had strong things to say about the Old Testament. He regarded it with a great deal more respect than many Christians today. His basis of respect was not simply that the Scriptures pointed to himself. He seemed to regard the Scriptures themselves as valuable—and more than that, as

unbreakable. What does this mean for us today as believers?

What does this mean for the Old Testament's portrayal of God?

14. "If you break even the *tiniest* one of these commandments—and if you teach others to do the same—oh, you'll be called the *tiniest* in the kingdom of heaven. But if you practice—and teach—these commands, you will be great in the kingdom of heaven." Boy, it sure seems like Jesus is teaching legalism. But from the context of his other sermons (and even the rest of this one, where he lays down an impossible standard), we know better. Yet it might be helpful to define legalism if we are to understand Jesus's words.

So what is legalism? Legalism is *not* adherence to rules. Legalism is mistaking the form of the rule for its substance, and abandoning the substance of the rule in favor of its form. That is to say, if I were to gossip about someone and say "I haven't disobeyed the command not to murder," I would be following the *form* of the law "do not murder," but not the *substance*—"do not hate your brother in your heart." So ironically, if I abandoned legalism and followed the heart of God, I would actually be adhering *more* strictly to the law and have an even *tougher* set of commands to follow as a result. By following the heart of God, I am actually falling under the weight of commands that are much more difficult to obey. In light of this, what does Jesus's statement, "I tell you the truth, unless your righteousness exceeds that of the Pharisees, you will never enter the kingdom of heaven" mean?

15. Jesus clearly has expectations for us as believers—yet he clearly and repeatedly states that we are saved by faith in him, not by adhering to those commands. What is the basis of obedience, then? Why even give the commands? We're saved either way, right?

16. The kingdom of God—that is, his kingship—places a great deal of weight on pleasing God. What are the reasons for this?

Knocking through the roof

Luke 5:17-26; Matthew 9:1-8; Mark 2:1-12

17. "Ask and you will receive" is often mistaken as an invitation to ask for anything you want. But if we check the context, Jesus seems to be saying something more specific. What is it?

18. "Seek and you will find." But see also Jeremiah 29:14b. What does God do in order to make sure our seeking is not in vain?

Why does God want us to "seek" in the first place?

19. "Knocking" in the context of the passage indicates persistence. Yet the door *will* be opened if we do it.

What does this indicate about God compared to the man in the parable who (at first) refuses to open the door?

20. Jesus is making an "if this, then how much more so that" argument here. If the man, begrudging as he was, would only open the door because of his friend's persistence, how much more so will God—who loves us—open the door for those who ask him! Yet from a spiritual standpoint, was does it mean to "knock"? What does it mean that "the door will be opened"?

21. Jesus was a compelling speaker who drew crowds. No doubt he was utterly enthralling to listen to. How would parables like this one facilitate his teaching? Name two ways.

22. Matthew thinks, "First this preacher told everyone they could never be good enough to enter the Kingdom of Heaven—and now all people have to do is ask, seek, knock? This man made no sense." Well? In the context of the Gospel, how does it make sense?

23. In what ways do the paralytic's friends epitomize the forwardness Jesus wants us to have with God?

24. "Friend, your sins are forgiven." Jesus prioritizes the condition of the soul over physical needs. His healing only comes *after* the fact of forgiveness. What does this tell us about God?

25. The authority of Jesus is on trial after he claims the man's sins are forgiven. What does he do to demonstrate his authority?

Although no one doubts Jesus's compassion, it is clear here that his healing is motivated by something else. What is it?

26. What is the point of commanding a paralyzed person to get up, take up his mat and walk? Since he's paralyzed, he can't follow the command—and since God is the one doing the healing, the man *still* has no power to follow the command! So why order him to get up?

The call of Matthew

Matthew 9:9-13; Mark 2:13-14; Luke 5:27-28

27. "'So enter through the narrow gate. For *wide* is the gate,' Jesus spread his arms, 'and broad is the road that leads to destruction—' he slammed a fist into his palm, '—and *many* enter through it.'
"Some in the crowd shifted their footing. Matthew spotted uneasy expressions. Why would Jesus be telling this to *them*? As Jews, weren't they already members of the kingdom?"
What is the point of telling this to those who are apparently saved?

What does this mean for us?

28. What does it mean that the way to destruction is wide while the way to salvation is narrow?

29. In this dramatization, why do you think Matthew follows Jesus?

Only the sick

Mark 2:15-17; Luke 5:29-32

30. Do you think the pharisee's mentality—that the company you keep reflects on you—has any merit? How so?

   If so, how is it different with Jesus?

31. Jesus describes those he is eating with as "the sick." This is judging them—and Jesus's hearers would understand that. Yet they would also understand that Jesus cares for them. How do you reconcile his love for these people with his designation of them?

32. "*You* have to come to *them*! Then they will come to God." Jesus is displaying a mentality that he will eventually ratify with the Great Commission. Why is this method of ministry—going out to the lost instead of waiting for them to come to you—more effective?

33. Charges are made against Jesus's character for his method of evangelism. How can we avoid falling

into the traps Jesus is accused of falling into—being polluted by the world (see James 1:27)—when we conduct missions work?

THE WHOM THE SCRIPTURES
TESTIFY • DEEPER STUDY

"In your anger do not sin." No one epitomizes this better than Jesus. He had hard things to say to hardheaded people— but rather than working against his anger, Jesus's love actually fueled his rage toward the pharisees.

How can we love the Scriptures without hating the stubbornness that comes from refusing the Scriptures? How can we love people without abhorring the stubbornness that destroys them? And when those who should know better are leading others astray, so that both are destroyed in the process—shouldn't we get upset?

God created the emotion of anger for a reason. And it's not so we can placidly sit by while outrageous things are done and stubborn people have their way. There will be justice.

Jesus finally goes head-to-head with the Pharisees here. The catalyst is a healed man who, instead of being grateful, immediately betrays Jesus. Later we will see another beggar by another pool (from John 9). That one will make the decision to side with Jesus—but this one sides with the pharisees. Physical healing is just that; it does not change the heart.

Yet it is clear Jesus still loves the beggar. It is also obvious from his entreaties to the Pharisees that he is frustrated at their unbelief. This frustration seems implausible if he has no concern for them. On the contrary— he loves them more than they can imagine.

Note: Due to the length of this dramatization, you may find it better to split this session into two studies.

A Prophet like me

Deuteronomy 18:14-19

1. What does Moses mean when he says "like me"? Besides events in his early life, what traits do Moses and Jesus have in common?

2. One of Moses's roles was to be an emissary to the Israelites, speaking the words of God. The Israelites could not bear the fire and smoke of God's presence—so they needed a human to converse with them. How does the incarnation fulfill this?

3. Moses's successor would lead the Israelites into the promised land. The successor's name was Joshua, a variant of *Yeshua*, or Jesus. How does this foreshadow Jesus?

Fleeing Bethlehem

Matthew 2:13-18

4. There's an irony here. God sent his Messiah to save the world, but the Messiah must be saved from Herod's wrath first. Why didn't God just save Jesus by stopping the slaughter of the children of Bethlehem?

Floating on the Nile

Exodus 2:1-4

5. Hindsight is 20/20—but in the moment, the right course of action is not always clear. Would you have done what Jochebed did? Why or why not?

Returning to Israel

Matthew 2:19-21

6. What is the basis of Joseph and Mary's return to Israel?

Returning to Egypt

Exodus 4:18-20

7. It must have been a great act of faith for Moses to return to Egypt. How does his return mirror Joseph's return?

By the Pool at Bethesda

John 5:1-9, 13

8. The Pool at Bethesda was most likely a Mikveh—a public pool used for ceremonial cleansing. What is the significance of this pool being related to healing?

9. Do you think the other Israelites frequenting the pool had a duty to help all the crippled beggars get into it? Why or why not?

He will carry our infirmities

Isaiah 53:4

10. What does it mean for us that the Messiah, more than simply healing us, will carry our infirmities upon his shoulders?

Jesus heals the infirm beggar

John 5:1-9, 13

11. "They're always here, aren't they. Waiting." In a more symbolic sense, what are the beggars really waiting for?

12. "Usually people have to bring their sick to Jesus—not the other way around." As is repeatedly established throughout the Gospels, Jesus knows the hearts of others. Therefore, he would know the heart

of this beggar—and that the infirm fellow would betray Jesus instead of following him. There are countless beggars by the gate, each in desperate need of Jesus's healing...and the sick are everywhere. So why does Jesus choose this one?

How does Jesus's behavior here influence our own attitudes in missions?

13. Jesus mentions that the Israelites wandered 40 years in the desert before being led into the Promised Land. How does that situation (and its related events) compare to the healing at the Pool of Bethesda (and its related events)?

14. Again, Jesus asks someone to do something that is physically impossible for them to do. What is the point of asking them to obey before healing them?

What can we apply from this?

15. Why does Jesus slip away into the crowd?

The beggar is questioned

John 5:9-13

16. Why is it significant that the beggar diverts responsibility for his actions?

Witnesses to Jesus's identity

John 5:14-47

This will not be the last Sabbath controversy—not by a long shot. However, it appears to be one of the earliest. Jesus's initial argument was based on his own nature in relation to the Father, while his subsequent arguments (in future episodes) were based on the nature of the Sabbath and the law. The focus of this argument becomes, as is often the case in John, centered on the identity of Jesus.

17. That Jesus found the beggar later indicates Jesus was looking for him—and not the other way around. Again, why spend so much time on someone who clearly is not making an effort to follow you? Jesus knows the beggar's heart—and he knows the man will sell him out as soon as he learns the name of his healer. Why does Jesus look for him?

18. "Stop sinning. Otherwise something worse might happen to you." This implies that the beggar's condition was a result of his sin. Read John 5:14 and 1st Corinthians 11:29-32. Compare these passages to John 9:1-3. Many Christians today commonly assume that illness is never a result of God's judgment—but the Bible indicates otherwise. Meanwhile, other people seem to believe that every illness must be a sign that the person is sinning. Based on these three passages, what is the truth of the matter?

Always at work
19. Compare Hebrews 4:1-11 to John 5:17. Clearly God is *always* at work, and all creation is continually

upheld by him. So in what sense did God rest in Genesis 2:3?

20. More will be discussed on the nature of the Sabbath in another study. For now, read Psalm 95:10-11. In the context of the Israelites wandering through the desert 40 years in unbelief and never entering the "rest" of God (in that case, the Promised Land), what is the true "rest" of God for believers?

The Son can do nothing by himself

Now we are getting into the real debate—the identity of Jesus.

21. "I'm sure you manage [the miracles] somehow." One might marvel at the stubbornness of this Pharisee—but aren't there people today who rationalize away miracles in the very same way? What do you think is behind this mentality?

22. "The Son can do nothing by himself." Instead, the sun is dependent upon what the Father shows him. The trinity is complex—but this aspect of the relationship has a theological basis that we can apply as believers. What is it?

23. The claim that "the Father loves the Son" is immediately followed by the concept of the Father showing the Son everything he does. Based on John 5:19, what is the point of the Father "showing" the Son anything? How would love motivate this?

24. Honoring Jesus is equated with honoring the one who sent him. Meanwhile, belief in Jesus is also equated with belief in the one who sent him. Why?

25. Jesus claims that those who believe in him have crossed over from death to life. But then he claims that after the resurrection, "those who have done good will rise to live, and those who have done evil will rise to be condemned." This appears to be based on their deeds rather than their belief or nonbelief in Jesus. What is Jesus saying?

26. "My judgment is just—for I seek not to please myself but him who sent me." How does that make his judgment just? How would the lack of that make judgment unjust?

27. The revelation here is that although Jesus has been tasked with judgment by the Father, he judges only as he hears—and he can only do what the Father shows him. In fact, he can do nothing apart from the Father. What does this imply regarding judgment?

The witnesses are called

Let's be fair to the pharisees. From their perspective, Jesus is a loon claiming to be equal to God. Imagine if somebody came up to you making that kind of claim. You would think they were crazy too.

But what if they gave evidence? Jesus didn't expect the Pharisees to blindly believe him. He summons witnesses to defend his identity.

28. Why does Jesus bother giving evidence for his identity? Shouldn't we all just have faith?

29. "If I testify about myself, my testimony is not valid." Jesus is speaking here under terms of Jewish law—that no one could testify on their own behalf. This statement signifies that the conversation is entering the legal arena, so to speak (otherwise, other factors allow his own testimony to be valid—see John 8:14). What follows will be reminiscent of a courtroom drama. Why subject his case for divinity to the standards of Jewish law?

30. I have heard it said that we should not use evidence to prove Christianity, because that is like putting Jesus on trial and making man the judge. In this scene, Jesus is literally putting himself on trial! Jesus then calls forth the Scriptures, the Father, John the Baptist and Jesus's own deeds as witnesses—thereby employing all shades of apologetics, from presuppositional to evidential, for his human opponents to assess. And yet, his authority as the judge is not diminished in any capacity for this. Instead, one could argue that the pharisees and others will now be judged *more* harshly for having rejected this evidence. In fact, the incarnation itself is a condescension to our level so we can see and ascertain God. Furthermore, it is on the basis of denying what Jesus has proven to them that the Pharisees will be judged. In that case, by putting himself on trial before us, God has actually *heightened* his authority to judge us. So the claim that we should not "put Jesus on trial" makes no sense—how else do we assess belief in him? Instead, we

should follow Jesus's example when speaking to nonbelievers—even those who stubbornly refuse to believe, like these Pharisees. In the case of John 5:31-47, how can we follow Jesus's example?

31. "Not that I accept human testimony, of course. I mention it that you might be saved—that's all." This displays a pragmatic mindset. How should we apply this mindset in evangelism?

32. John writes that Jesus came "full of grace and truth." Yet here, Jesus says, "you have never heard his voice nor seen his form, and his Word *clearly* does not dwell in you." Try saying that to the people you know, and see if they call you gracious. Ah, but perhaps "grace" is defined differently in the Bible than in American culture. How does the Bible define "full of grace"? And where does "truth" fit in?

33. Studying the Scriptures (dwelling in the Word, so to speak) is differentiated from having God's Word dwell in *you*. Bearing in mind John 5:39-40, what is the defining difference?

34. Besides his ability to peer into their hearts, name three ways Jesus knows the Pharisees do not have the love of God in their hearts—simply based off this conversation.

How might you struggle with those same problems today?

35. "You, who study the Scriptures so often! But you refuse to see what they clearly spell out—the true nature of the Messiah!" The Pharisees, like many people today, miss the true nature of the Messiah. Why couldn't the Pharisees see it?

36. "No, your accuser is Moses, on whom your hopes are set." Obviously Moses isn't going to be the one judging them. So in context, what does this mean?

37. Jesus's face starts turning a deep crimson. After that much anger and frustration, blood is rushing to his face. We often don't think of the human component of Jesus's incarnation—but it's there. We also neglect that part of Jesus's ministry is to set an example for us. No doubt his words here would have been seen as disrespectful—but he never sinned. How can we follow Jesus's example here?

QUESTIONS IN THE NIGHT •

DEEPER STUDY

We all have questions. That night, Nicodemus had no peace. He needed to know the identity of the man who was turning his world upside-down.

How many of us have been drawn to the character of Jesus—to knowing more of who he is? Even as an unbeliever, Nicodemus displayed the curiosity in Jesus's identity. After all, that is our purpose in life. To know more of who God is—and to be known by the God who so loved us that he gave his one and only Son.

The Bronze Serpent

Numbers 21:4-9

1. It is not enough to say the Israelites simply didn't trust that God loved them. What kind of God says, "Oh, so you don't believe I love you? I'm going to kill you in a painful way until you believe I love

you!" No, their sin here was much greater. What was the real problem with their attitude?

2. Do you think the Israelite's complaints deserved the consequence God gave them? Why or why not?

3. Even after God presented his solution, the people still needed to "look at it and live" in order to be saved from the snakebites (the consequences of their sin). Why is this important?

4. God's provision may seem strange—it is something the people can look at, as opposed to faith in the invisible God. God prohibits worshiping idols, so how does it benefit God to provide something physical for people to turn to as a provision for their sins?

5. "Slow to anger, and abounding in love." It is moments like these that spark this description of Yahweh. God is slow to anger—but he does get angry. Yet the emphasis here is on God's mercy. Modern readers might see in this some "angry God of the Old Testament." But the ancient readers would have seen an example of the merciful God of history—abounding in love. What is the difference in mindset that causes them to see it differently from some modern readers?

Nicodemus meets with Jesus (p1)

John 3:1-10

6. "*No one* can see the Kingdom of God unless he is born again." Why does Jesus go straight to this?

7. In terms of mindset and lifestyle, what does "born again" entail?

   How does this apply to us as believers?

8. "The Spirit, like the wind, is not so easy to predict or understand—and neither are those born again." In this context, how is the Spirit difficult to predict or understand?

9. Jesus loves speaking in metaphors. He knows that those who believe in him will understand him through the spirit (my sheep will hear my voice). In addition to separating the wheat from the chaff, he also speaks this way in order to make you think about what he is saying. How might this be an effective teaching strategy?

10. Why emphasize that "it's clearly a redemption from their sins—not simply their earthly enemies"?

I will give them a heart of flesh

Ezekiel 36:24-29a

11. Who are the Israelites really being saved from?

12. Read Galatians 5:5, 16, 22-23; Jeremiah 32:38-40. How does God move us to follow his decrees?

Nicodemus meets with Jesus (p2)

John 3:11-15

13. In the context of the Ezekiel passage, what does it mean to be born again?

14. Rather than being ignored or nullified, the law sets the terms for Jesus's mission on Earth. What are those terms?

What, then, is one way Jesus fulfills the law?

For God so loved the world: The Passover

John 3:16-21; Exodus 12:1-13

15. What was God's reason for the incarnation?

16. There's an irony here. When God comes during the Passover, the goal is *not* that he should come to you,

but that you should be "passed over" through the blood of the lamb. Otherwise, you will perish. But now God comes in the flesh—as Jesus—and the goal is to come to him…or else perish. The crazy part is that you are perishing *apart* from Jesus for the exact same reasons you are perishing *from* God's presence (without the blood). What is the defining difference? How does this difference tie together the two events?

17. There is a holy fear of Yahweh here. The Israelites know they are in God's good graces—yet they still paint their doorposts. How might we as believers benefit by recalling that holy fear?

18. "This is the verdict: light has come into the world—but men loved darkness instead of light, because their deeds were evil." John is commenting on the reason for unbelief. He does not see ignorance or intellectuality as the primary obstacle. Instead, what is the problem in John's eyes?

Where do you see this today?

19. How does knowing God's purpose for the incarnation help us understand Jesus's identity?

OVERVIEW OF PARTS 1-6

LET'S BRING IT ALL TOGETHER

1. What major parts of Jesus's character have been shown from these dramatizations?

2. What recurring themes have you spotted? Name at least three.

3. In what ways have you been challenged or convicted?

BIBLIOGRAPHY & NOTES

01 • A Voice in the Desert

A Voice in the Desert

1. John preaches repentance:
   John 1:1-34; Luke 3:1-18

2. Malachi chastises the people:
   Overview of Malachi, particularly 1:1-14; 2:1-9, 17;
   3:1

3. The baptism of Jesus:
   Matthew 3:1-17; Mark 1:1-11; Luke 3:21-23

4. Isaiah 42:1 is quoted in the final section.

02 • The Temptation of Jesus

Jesus is tempted in the desert

1. Temptation #1: Stone to Bread:
   Matthew 4:1-3; Mark 1:12-13; Luke 4:1-3

2. …But on every word:
    Deuteronomy 8:1-5

3. Temptation #2: Leap of Faith:
    Matthew 4:4-6; Luke 4:4, 9-10

4. Testing at Meribah:
    Deuteronomy 6:16; Exodus 17:1-7

5. Temptation #3: All the Kingdoms:
    Matthew 4:7-11; Luke 4:12, 5-8, 13

6. Isaiah 42:6-7 is quoted in the final section.

03 • Too Small a Thing

Jesus and the woman at the well

1. Jonah's anger at God:
    Jonah 4; also refers to 2:9

2. Jesus at the well with Sariah:
    John 4:4-26

3. The name of the woman at the well is never given, so I picked a good name from a list of common names in 1st century Samaria.

4. Jonah talks with Amos:
    Amos 3:2, 8; 4:4-11, 13; 5:14; 7:4-6, 10-15; 9:9-12

5. See also 2nd Kings 14:25; Genesis 48:5-6; 2nd Samuel 14:14

6. The Bible never mentions Jonah speaking with Amos. However, it is a fair extrapolation, as they both prophesied at the same time and Amos would be known to Jonah as the prophet from Tekoa. It is plausible Jonah would have sought Amos's company at some point, especially after his experiences. As always, I have endeavored to stay

true to their personalities. The passages referred to show up in their conversation.

7. Sariah tells the town about Jesus:
    John 4:39-42

8. Too Small a Thing (Servant Song):
    Isaiah 49:5-6

04 • A Prophet without Honor

The rejection of Jesus at Nazareth

1. Flashback: Jesus at the Temple:
    Luke 2:41-52

2. Referenced verses include Isaiah 61:1-3a; Psalm 142:7; Jeremiah 5:25; Micah 5:2; Isaiah 2:1-5; Micah 4:1-5; Isaiah 65:25; Isaiah 49:6 (alluded to by Jesus).

3. Reunion with the family:
    See notes below

4. Some kind of reunion occurred (obviously Jesus wouldn't ignore his own family), but it is not detailed in Scripture. Therefore, all the details in this section of the dramatization are interpolated from various sources, ranging from archeology (the stove, ancient carpentry, etc.) to the books of James and Jude (for their respective personalities) and Mark 6:3 (for the names of Jesus's brothers, the apparent early death of Joseph—and Jesus's previous occupation as carpenter). Jesus's conversation with Mary is greatly influenced by Luke 1:46-56; 2:19, 33-35; 22:41-44, along with a general study of their personalities as the Gospels portray them.

5. The Stone the Builders Rejected:
   Psalm 118:21-23

6. Rejection at Nazareth:
   Luke 4:14-30

05 • For the Sake of the Call

The call of the first disciples

1. Elisha is called by Elijah:
   1st Kings 19:19-21

2. You have to count the cost!:
   Luke 9:57-62; 14:25-35

3. As a traveling preacher, Jesus repeated his messages often. The Bible often mentions him teaching but does not mention what he is teaching. Since we can assume that the Gospels give us a complete record of all the subject material Jesus taught, he must have been teaching something from one of the four Gospels. Thus throughout the dramatizations, I will frequently insert material from other passages in areas where Jesus is recorded as "teaching." The passages I select will usually tie into the narrative (though not necessarily).

4. Call of the disciples:
   Luke 5:1-11

5. See also Matthew 4:18-22; Mark 1:14-20.

06 • The Mission of Jesus

Casting out the demoniac in Luke 4:31-37

1. Praying in the morning:
   Luke 5:16 (see also 4:42)

2. Isaiah before Ahaz:
   Isaiah 9:1-7

3. Casting out the demon in the synagogue:
   Luke 4:31-37

4. The teaching here is from the Matthean beatitudes found in Matthew 5:3-12.

5. Jesus references Jeremiah 9:23-24; Psalm 147:10-11; Isaiah 66:2b

07 • Savior of the Unclean

The call of Matthew and related events

1. I pronounce you clean:
   13:38-39, 45; 14:1-7

2. Notice that the rest of the ritual (after 14:7) is not included. I wanted to highlight the part where the man is pronounced clean and show what that entailed.

3. Matthew's debate:
   The passage being read is Numbers 5:1-3

4. No one really knows Matthew's past. However, his familiarity with the Scriptures indicate some kind of past with it, and the fact that he is a tax collector at the time Jesus calls him means he was in a bad position with the Israelites. To willingly choose that profession with so much knowledge of Scripture indicates total disenfranchisement. Add to this that he was ready to follow Jesus and you have someone who was searching but had given up thinking he would ever find anything.

5. Most of the statements made summarize scriptural themes rather than quoting passages. The only unscriptural statements made are a) the messiah is

for those who keep the law (it's the opposite!); b) that those suffering permanently from skin diseases have done some great sin (or their parents), so their eternally unclean status is merited; and c) that the rabbi is somehow clean enough for God.

6. Although the law gave a provision until the coming of Christ Jesus, it didn't actually take away sin. It merely covered it over, the way a credit card covers over debt but doesn't actually pay for it. By offering sacrifices *in faith*, they swiped that credit card. In a sense, they were displaying faith in the coming sacrifice. God in his forbearance left the sins committed beforehand unpunished, until the times should reach their fulfillment. Or to put it another way, then Jesus came along and paid off the credit card's account.

7. Regarding disease as a result of sin, Jesus acknowledges this as a possibility—but makes it clear that sometimes other factors may be at work. Paul echoes this later, but neither supports the idea that all disease is a result of sin. (Though to go the other direction and say that *no* disease is a result of sin would be unscriptural as well!)

8. Some of my favorite passages on the subjects raised include the following:

9. God is holy:
   Leviticus 20:26; see also 1st Peter 1:15-16

10. Lex Taliones (The Retribution Principle):
    Exodus 21:24; see also Obadiah 1:15

11. • No pleasure in the death of the wicked:
    Ezekiel 33:11; see also 2nd Peter 3:9

12. If you are willing:
    Luke 5:12-15; Matthew 8:1-4; Mark 1:40-45

13. We know from extrabiblical sources that the Roman soldiers did not treat Israelites well. We also know—both from the Bible and other historical sources—that tax collectors were regarded about the same as a defector.

14. Jesus's sermon is from Matthew 5:17-20.

15. The "I need to preach in other towns" line is from Luke 4:43.

16. Knocking through the roof:
    Luke 5:17-26; Matthew 9:1-8; Mark 2:1-12

17. Jesus's sermon is from Luke 11:5-13. (See also Matthew 7:7-11.)

18. The call of Matthew:
    Matthew 9:9-13; Mark 2:13-14; Luke 5:27-28

19. Jesus's sermon is from Matthew 7:12-14.

20. Only the sick:
    Mark 2:15-17; Luke 5:29-32

21. Some of the comments made by the Pharisees and Jesus's response to them are loose quotations of Luke 7:31-34. Don't worry—I'll include "But wisdom is proved right by her children" (Luke 7:35) in a later dramatization.

08 • To Whom the Scriptures Testify

John 5—The man by the pool at Bethesda and the ensuing conflict

1. A Prophet like me:
   Deuteronomy 18:14-19

2. Fleeing Bethlehem:
   Matthew 2:13-18

3. Floating on the Nile:
   Exodus 2:1-4

4. Returning to Israel:
   Matthew 2:19-21

5. Returning to Egypt:
   Exodus 4:18-20

6. By the Pool at Bethesda:
   John 5:1-9, 13

7. He will carry our infirmities:
   Isaiah 53:4

8. Jesus heals the infirm beggar:
   John 5:1-9, 13

9. The beggar is questioned:
   John 5:9-13

10. Witnesses to Jesus's Identity:
    John 5:14-47

11. This will not be the last Sabbath controversy—not by a long shot. However, it appears to be one of the earliest. Jesus's initial argument was based on his own nature in relation to the Father, while his subsequent arguments (in future episodes) were based on the nature of the Sabbath and the law. The focus of this argument becomes, as is often the case in John, centered on the identity of Jesus.

09 • Questions in the Night

Nicodemus meets with Jesus

1. The Bronze Serpent:
   Numbers 21:4-9

2. Nahshon son of Amminadab is the representative of Judah in Numbers 7. It made sense for him to be

complaining here as the main representative for Israel, as he brought the sacrifice on the first day (Numbers 7:12) and therefore has a prominent position among the tribes. This also occasioned the location of the bronze serpent as the camp of Judah.

3. Nicodemus meets with Jesus p1: John 3:1-10

4. Jesus says, "My sheep will hear my voice." This language is from John 10:27.

5. Throughout these dramatizations, Jesus will say "Jesus-isms" that can be found throughout Scripture. I will probably not highlight these, as doing so would be tedious. "Seek and you will find" is one example in this dramatization. Jesus also alludes to Jeremiah 29:13-14a ("I will always come to those who search"). He often alludes to Scripture, and some of these allusions will not be mentioned in this bibliography. I generally try to phrase Jesus's speech with themes that are familiar to his other statements in the Gospels or to the Scriptures he would have known by heart.

6. I will give them a heart of flesh: Ezekiel 36:24-29a

7. Nicodemus meets with Jesus p2: John 3:11-15

8. Jesus quotes Ecclesiastes 7:11, Psalm 14:1b (and therefore Psalm 53:1b)—and Isaiah 53:6a.

9. For God so loved the world: The Passover: John 3:16-21; Exodus 12:1-13

10. The portrayal of Pharaoh is based on Exodus 11:9-10.

A NOTE FROM THE AUTHOR

I remember looking up at the stars on a cold night when I was little, thinking, "God is so COOL!" More than anything else, God's coolness fascinates me. His holy wrath is awe-inspiring, his grace brings tears to my eyes…but his coolness came first. He is the alpha and omega.

God created us with the purpose of bringing glory to him. We are here to love and be loved by God. And that is what I want my life to be. I want to be remembered for highlighting who God is.

So how do I do that? I highlight the things that appeal to me most about God. His cool creation—fungi, planets, geology. His awesome character—found in every ounce of the Bible. By learning about God's creation, I learn about God.

But I also learn about him from my failings. I struggle with anxiety, to the point where I could be paralyzed by it. God has been the real source of peace for me—because he forgives me and reminds me that I don't accomplish things by my own power. All that I have accomplished he has done for me. The pressure's on God to fulfill my purpose. I am simply his vessel.

Of course, God has given me some wonderful gifts to help me along the way. My wife Nicole is the best of those, and she inspires me and brings me joy every day. It is truly a delight to be loved.

–Ian Vroon

Find Ian on his website at
https://isaiah2612.weebly.com/

Made in USA - Kendallville, IN
1204663_9798651286263
12 03 2020 0841